Out of Oregon

by

Tim Pedersen

Aaron + Hannah

You crazy kids inspire me!

Love ya.

– Tim

Cover art and photo by Tim Pedersen

ISBN-13: 978-1494995867
ISBN-10: 1494995867
Fiction
First Edition

Contact: timped2006@hotmail.com

To Kate, of course.
Without you, my Beloved, there
would be no adventure.

CONTENTS

Thanks to Aaron and Isaac for pointing out my grammar and continuity errors. Thanks to Shannon for all the coffee and for keeping me motivated. Thanks to Kate for being patient and encouraging. Thanks to William for thinking I'm funnier than I really am. Thanks to Grandpa for being my hero.

I don't mean to write just another road trip story. I told a friend of mine the other day that there are already too many of them and she disagreed. I guess everyone thinks they have a story to tell. And maybe they do, but I doubt they're all worth reading. She was probably just being nice.

Another friend has suggested that this book is more for me than for the reader, so it doesn't really matter what I say or whether anyone bothers to pick it up. He may be right, but I still hope that what I've thought about and experienced are relatable and that one or two readers will walk away with some insight that they hadn't considered before. That's everyone's hope, probably. We used to want to be firefighters and cowboys. Now everyone just wants to be remembered for something. To be quoted, really. Maybe that's the result of the world getting smaller and more connected. I can't decide if it's a more noble ambition, or less. I think the best quotes come from people who don't know their statement is going to be remembered. Or don't care if it is. Significantly, in a world that is becoming more concerned with fame, quotes by celebrities are more likely considered to be true. I can't back that up, and I don't resent anyone for it. It just seems there's a growing trend to quote movie stars when arguing a point. Perhaps it's because they're experts in the art of eloquence. Their job requires it, after all. Maybe people are more captivated by ideas today than by facts. Maybe they always were. I can't say I'm not a romantic when it's the right time of day, and when the windows are open, and the weather is a certain way, and the smells are just right, and so on.

I think I digress, but I never had a point to make, so maybe not.

Growing up, I was always afraid I wouldn't have any stories

to tell my kids. It really had nothing to do with having kids just like a "bucket list" has nothing to do with dying. Who knows if I'll even have children. Really, I was just afraid of being boring. I doubt I could have honestly answered at the time why or to whom I wanted to be interesting. It just seemed like a good thing. Part of the problem was that I didn't realize most of the stories my friends told were lies. Nobody has an exciting life when they're seven.

I had a similar conversation with a guy several years ago. He wanted to work with troubled kids, but confided in me that he was afraid he didn't have any good stories. I remember thinking at the time that it was a bizarre concern. Essentially, he thought he wouldn't have any credibility without having been through some of what they were dealing with. Later on, I was guilty of the same fear, although for selfish reasons.

I had traveled a little after high school, but never without an agenda. I won't bore you with the details because I'm bored just thinking about it.

It must have been around mid-September of 2004 that I ran out of money and supporters and had to come home to work for a living. It's easy to convince old people to give you money to travel if you're doing charitable work or spreading religion, but I just wanted to fly from country to country and eat the strange food and see the irrelevant, old buildings. At least, that was how I felt about it. I had seen a lot of the world very comfortably, which is the worst way to travel.

A few months into holding two miserable jobs at once, I was discussing with a friend what it means to have an adventure. Or, rather, what must happen for it to be called an adventure. See, I come from a generation who uses language more to shock and impress than to convey accuracy. It's not uncommon to hear of an "adventure" to the coffee shop or the grocery store. And, after the tale is told, the hearer is usually left wanting for the element of adventure of which the story initially gave promise. A foolproof way to tell how dull someone's life is, I've found, is to pay attention to how hard they try to convince others that they're "living the dream." It could just be that I have a bad attitude and these people are just trying to make the mundane seem exciting. Who knows?

Several weeks later, upon recalling this conversation, I realized that I'd never had a true adventure. It also became quickly apparent as I considered what we'd talked about that I would only find adventure if I shoved off in my present state (broke, bored, and unmotivated) rather than saving up enough money and enthusiasm to ensure that nothing would take me out of my comfort zone while on the road. That being what we settled on as the definition of an adventure: an event that rips you from your comfort zone and forces you to come up with a way to find food and shelter and press onward to wherever you will go - whether you plan on going there or not.

As I rolled the idea over in my head for another month or two, I tried my best not to make plans. If I planned a trip, I would be found in the same state in which I'd set off on my previous voyages around the world - prepared. It was always a blessing to be prepared before leaving town when the goal was for nothing to go wrong. This trip would have to be different from the start.

I was embarrassed by the notion of it all because I knew anyone who found out what my plan (or lack thereof) was would try to be the voice of reason. My dad would want to know all of the details and my grandparents would offer to donate whatever money I hadn't been able to come up with. They wouldn't understand if I told them that part of the adventure was in being impoverished and not having an agenda. That is a bizarre concept when you come from a small, close-knit family who takes care of each other. And never being one to defend my actions when a critic appeared who held my safety as the first priority or who had a loud opinion about how "you can't just sleep on park benches," I had made a habit in my life of pretending to agree with "better ideas." It makes more sense sometimes to be polite and do your own thing anyway than to try to convince someone of something that is, in the end, your choice and that the consequences of which will only affect you. This was before I learned not to care about what people think. Maybe the very intention of seeking out an adventure was adventurous because I was very uncomfortable with all of it.

Because I was so uncomfortable with the idea, I may have never taken the plunge, but was spared from spending the rest of my life in the "non-planning" stage (I know people who have been planning trips for years but will never go because a vehicle breakdown or a move to a new apartment always drains the bank account) by a run-in with an old high school acquaintance at some divey bar of which I'm proud to have forgotten the name.

I had just gotten off work, and rather than go home to my parents' house, I had a habit of killing time at the bar until I was sure they would be in bed and I wouldn't have to tell them about my day. It was always reminiscent of coming home from elementary school and answering the same questions as the day before.

"How was work?"

"Fine."

"Do anything exciting?"

"Nope...same stuff as yesterday."

I didn't mean to be dismissive. There was really just nothing to say that hadn't already been discussed several times. To make matters worse, I wasn't convinced they wanted to know the details of my dead end job. It was just a way to feel connected (Later on, I would realize that in your 20s, the parent/child relationship reverses and it becomes the kids responsibility to make the parents feel loved and appreciated). After discussing the weather, the simplest topic of small-talk is work. To this day, I don't know why anyone would want to spend their time thinking and talking about work after it's time to go home, but most people will beat the subject to death whenever they run into an acquaintance or old friend.

On this night, a familiar face that I hadn't seen in a few years was sitting at the other end of the bar. I thought he was overdressed for the atmosphere and that he probably thought everyone else in the room was under-dressed. Later, I would learn that he had a policy of looking put together whenever he went out because it affected how people treated him, and usually for the better. He met most of his girlfriends by being the best-dressed guy in the bar. Of course, it never worked out in the long run because he met most of his girlfriends at a bar. I've been told that the best place to meet a wife is at the grocery store. Who knows? Every successful couple will tell you that their way is the best. I've talked to couples who dated for a dozen years and couples who were married within two months of meeting. They all recommend doing things their way.

Now, when one lives in a small town, there are a few tricks one must employ if one ever wants to get anything done. If you stop and catch up every time you run into someone you know, you'd really never accomplish what you were around town to do.

Greg was drunk when we ran into each other at Billy's, or Chuck's, or whatever the place was called. If his inhibitions had been in tact, he may have cooperated in pretending not to see me like the rest of the people in the room who knew me and we probably would never have started talking. Even if we had, I probably wouldn't have felt comfortable telling him about what had been dominating my thoughts over the last few weeks and months.

Sometimes I have anxiety. But, I think anxiety is only a

manifestation of pride. Or at least my version of anxiety. It happens when I'm too concerned about my own well being or reputation and it eats away at my ability to function. I think a happy pill is the last thing I need under these circumstances. Rather a dose of reality and a reminder that the world is bigger than me has always brought me around. I've heard it said that getting outside is a wonderful substitute for Serotonin re-uptake inhibitors. Anxiety is a self-fulfilling prophecy, I think. It makes you late for work and then you get fired, giving you something to be anxious about.

The rest of the time I'm laid back. Almost to a fault. When I get like this, I don't care about the things I should care about - or anything else. Times like these, I find humor in everything and it drives my mom crazy. I don't know if she's right for caring about important things, or if I'm right for not taking things too seriously. There's probably some in-between option that we would both do well to drag ourselves towards.

Maybe I'm bipolar, but then I think that's just another word that doctors use to categorize people. Somewhere along the line, someone decided that humans shouldn't have a range of emotions and called it a disease when they do. Most people would disagree with me and would win the argument because I don't have data to back up my position. It only makes sense to me. People put too much faith in doctors, I guess. And doctors probably feel the same way. The brain is a mystery and, unfortunately, is responsible for most of what our bodies do. That makes most of human nature a mystery, if I'm not mistaken. I should probably just read more books.

Now that I think back on it, we may have only started talking because he thought I was someone else. Or maybe he just calls everybody Jeff, which is not my name.

After talking for a while about what we'd been up to for the last couple of years, and after more than a couple beers, I could tell that Greg wouldn't try to talk me out of packing up my car and heading East in search of trouble. He was no stranger to getting into trouble. Greg was the kid in school who was always on the radar, not because he was dumb and criminal, but because he was bored and anything nonacademic that a student does to entertain himself is against the rules. This was probably a sign of intelligence if anything. That's what they always say on those talk shows where dumb people sit on a chair in front of a live studio audience and bring their marital problems before the some celebrity doctor and the rest of the world.

Anyway, whatever Greg usually found to entertain himself was looked down upon. Like putting dish soap in the fountain and turning the courtyard into a foam pit. In the name of science, of course. Teachers don't understand. It's just a job for them and any inconvenience is, well, an inconvenience. I was once arrested for pulling a childish prank and the cops told me that they used to do the same thing all the time when they were kids. It's not very comforting to know that what you've done is only illegal because you were born 30 years too late. Or 30 years too early, in other cases.

I mentioned to him that I was bored with my jobs and living in my parents' upstairs and that I really just wanted to take a trip somewhere - an adventure. I was a little embarrassed when I couldn't answer any of his questions about the details, but it quickly became apparent that he wasn't judging me for not having a plan. In fact, if I hadn't already been intending to go, he probably would have talked me into a few weeks on the road. Some people have a natural gift for projecting their dreams onto anyone they run into. Maybe people like this seek out impressionable types. I'm not admitting that I'm impressionable, but I tend not to argue.

Greg was getting excited at the idea of having an adventure. The more we schemed about what each of us would do if given the opportunity, the faster he talked and the more serious he seemed. I, on the other hand, was getting scared because it was looking like I would have to deliver. I didn't stay scared, of course, once I realized that I'd found the avenue I was looking for to get out of town and find my adventure. I think Greg had different motivations as he kept mentioning that he wanted to get fired from his restaurant job.

I wish I could recall the discussion that led to us deciding we'd leave in one week, but the memory of that night is fuzzy. I can remember the shirt the bartender was wearing, the smell of rain, and spilling the last gulp of my third beer (which offended Greg very much - he liked beer), but he and I have had too many talks to remember the exact words of our most defining conversation.

However it happened, the plan (as much as we tried not to have one) was to leave Dallas in a few days and whatever wasn't prepared by then wasn't important. I should mention that we're not from the thriving metropolis of Dallas, Texas, but rather the lesser-known wide spot in the road called Dallas, Oregon. Whenever I was out of state or country, I would tell people that I was from Salem, Oregon to avoid having the same conversation.

Greg, like myself, wasn't tied down by a "real" job or a mortgage. What he did have was a girlfriend who he wasn't serious about because the relationship was rather one-sided, and being under the influence, as he was, provided the perfect opportunity to cut things off. I'm usually very non-confrontational and, under any other circumstances, it would kill me to have to hear a guy dump his girl. Something about that night made the whole thing bearable, though, and I think I laughed harder hearing half of the conversation than I'd laughed in a month.

"Hi, Babe."

"..."

"No, I'm over here at _____ drinki– Who's that yelling in the background? Why are we yelling?"

"…"

"No...tell her – okay – no, tell her I'm not going to – wait...I don't think you'd know him...we went to high school together.

"..."

"Well, damn, Honey. I told you where I'd be – Why is this my problem?"

"...!"

"Okay. Well, yeah...don't worry about it."

"..."

And so forth.

Later Greg would tell me that their conversations always sounded like fights. I guess that made it easier to turn it into a fight when it was convenient. He also told me that he liked her well enough, but you'd be shooting yourself in the foot to go on an extended trip while attached to someone back home. Anyway, it was a good thing Greg dumped her, because he fell in love with every female we met on the road. He couldn't help it. Greg was Irish.

I wonder if "smitten" derives from the word "smite?" I'll have to ask my friend Isaac. He knows all about words. He's also a better writer than I, but less motivated, which makes all the difference.

two

I had a 1977 Ford Granada that my Uncle had given me out of pity when I returned from my latest voyage with no car, no job, and no money. Not the most romantic car to drive over the country in, but if it bothers you, maybe you should read Orwell or Kerouac.

I can't tell you the color, because there was no one color that covered more surface than another. I think it was navy blue from the factory. The tires were badly worn and the windshield was cracked. All four doors opened, but the rear doors had to be slammed if you wanted them to stay shut at 70 miles per hour (probably the result of years of being opened and closed furiously by children who didn't yet have the life experience to measure the amount of force they were exerting).

I named the car Dave because I had a tendency to kick dents into it and I would have felt bad assigning it a female name given the abuse.

After abusing Dave, I would always have a sinking feeling in my stomach. Then I would find a newspaper with used car ads thinking that if I started over with a different car, I would treat it better.

Still, Dave was a better option than anything Greg had to offer. He had a motorcycle and a cramped, red Toyota pickup. I vetoed both. Secretly I was hoping Dave would let us down halfway across the country and I'd be forced to upgrade to something I could be more proud of.

All I had to do was walk out on my jobs, scrape up some gas money, and throw a random assortment of "essentials" into Dave's trunk. I'd learned years before that it doesn't matter what you pack to take along on a trip. You won't use 80% of it and there will be several necessary items that you've forgotten. Now I just grab whatever looks appealing at the time, enough to fill a duffel bag, and I find I have about the same success rate.

Greg's strategy is more random than mine (if that's possible). He simply doesn't take anything that he hasn't used in the last 48 hours. It might actually make more sense, but there are obvious downfalls. It's for this reason that he forgot to bring socks.

We had to admit that we wouldn't get far without gas money. Food could be begged, borrowed, or stolen, but Dave was fickle and refused to run on dreams. The way I dug my feet into him, I would probably have gotten further and with less headaches if I'd traveled by horseback with a mean set of spurs.

I've always been amused by stories of people converting their car to run on fast food grease. It seems like you'd spend enough money on the conversion to drive across the country several times on gasoline. The irony is that if you have enough money to free yourself from a gas dependency, then you have enough money to just feed the dependency until a better option is manufactured. Of course, it's more a matter of principle. Which I can appreciate. I guess what I think is strange about it is that the same people won't go as far as to quit driving or quit wearing clothes made by children. Their sacrifice has to be convenient. It's like how vegetarians will buy meatless products that look and taste like meat because they agree that the pursuit of meat is noble - but only if nothing has to die. During a conversation once about just that, I asked a vegetarian friend if human-baby-flavored, imitation human baby meat would be ethical because no babies had to die. He wasn't amused.

Greg sold his motorcycle to a friend of his who had been trying to buy it for years. He'd regret it later, but with an adventure approaching, one never admits that it will eventually be over. A little basic math would have told us that the money from that sale would only put enough gas in Dave to get through five or six states. But, who knows what can happen in a couple thousand miles?

Money isn't as important as people think it is, anyway. I think currency was only invented as a system for cooperative people to feel like they're contributing to society. What I mean by that is: the more you refuse to pay for things, the more things you get for free - food, housing, healthcare...

And if you continue refusing to pay for things for long enough, you go to jail and get everything free for the rest of your life. Eventually, everyone will realize this and we'll run out of cooperative people.

Folks will do funny things for money, too. They'll get out of their warm beds at ungodly hours and drive across town to spend several hours doing what someone else wants them to do. I don't think it'll ever make sense to me, but even I cooperate. For now.

Upon hearing of our scheme, my parents realized that I was insane and offered up some charity in hopes that I wouldn't die of an empty gas tank. They were not travelers and were terribly afraid of the world. If I learned anything in all my travels, it was that wherever you go, the locals are at home and they don't think of themselves as foreign. Adults love to tell kids that "spiders are more afraid of you than you are of them," but they don't take their own advice.

~

Sometimes I do strange things because I think the world is interesting and it seems a waste to follow social rules all the time. I also do things that I'm afraid of because I have this idea that it will make me a better person. I may or may not be right about that, but I do.

I was working in a warehouse at the time, basically moving things from one part of the building to another. I can't imagine how the company made any money by paying me to do this, but I guess the business is still there today, so what do I know? The boss was a tyrant as always seems to be the case with warehouse gigs, and I imagined I'd quit very dramatically and leave as a hero. I'd walk into his office that overlooks the floor and say something I had prepared about corporate America getting the little man down and about how he himself had started at the bottom once upon a time - something very Martin Luther King Jr. He would be speechless and I would pee on his computer or something.

Anyway, it didn't turn out like that, and the reason I mention that I go against the grain sometimes is this: it scared me to think that I would leave without giving notice because, in our technological age, employers have ways of finding out if an applicant left their previous job well. As much as I didn't want to admit that I'd have to come home and find a job eventually, it was a reality, and I wanted to set myself up now to make that task easier then. Because I was afraid of leaving on a sour note, I forced myself to do just that. Not as sour as I would have liked for the sake of the story, but enough to scare myself. The boss was the only other person trained to do my job, whatever it was I accomplished, so I spent my last day moving each stack of product to exactly the wrong place. No one knew it was my last day at the time, but I wouldn't be coming back on Monday. Now that I've been back home and have found other jobs, I realize that my last day working for Mr. Hoyt didn't affect the rest of my life as much as I thought it would. It did, however, have the desired effect on my psyche. I learned to care about unimportant things just a little bit less.

My other job, I didn't entirely hate. The boss was more pleasant and I actually felt bad abandoning her. I didn't give her enough notice, but a couple days before we took off, I offered some pathetic excuse for why I wouldn't be available to work anymore. Dallas, Oregon is a small town and I'm sure she learned the truth within hours of our conversation, but she didn't mention it.

From the time of our chance encounter over beers to the day of our departure, Greg and I had pulled together a less than impressive wad of cash, but I couldn't tell you how much we were taking with us. It was no accident that we never counted it. While we hadn't agreed not to, I think we both knew that counting the money would be like starting a countdown of the days before we would be forced to turn towards home for lack of resources to push on. And not knowing what we had really freed us from worry. There was no number assigned to where we could go. It was liberating to ignorantly pretend that we had enough gas money to drive to Saturn.

Actually, I think he did drive us to Saturn one night while I was sleeping, but we came crashing down somewhere in Wyoming right about the time I woke up.

three

We left on a Sunday in February. I should mention that we only packed enough to fill the trunk. The idea was that we'd leave the back seat empty so we could lean the front seats back when it was time to sleep. It didn't quite work out like that, but it was a noble effort. Other than clothes and the like, we brought an outdated atlas of the lower 48, a camping stove, and various other non-essentials. My sister made us some mixed CDs, but she doesn't have very good taste in music which is ironic as she's married to a musician. I left them at the bottom of my bag rather than risk Greg's judgment.

"What should we put on..."Death Metal Mix #7," or "Bon Jovi's Greatest Hits?"

"I'd rather give myself a root canal," he would probably say. "That guy has never even won a Grammy."

He brought enough albums by bands I'd never heard of to drown out the road noise for months. Every true musician knows that the best way to spare yourself the condemnation of other musicians is to listen to unknown bands so that no one will be able to base their opinion of you on your musical taste.

Right after I acquired Dave, a 90 year old woman in a Buick turned across the front of me at one of the five stoplights in town. That knocked the body out of alignment with itself and the frame and, from then on, the wind came through every seam at speeds. On the plus side, it acted as a built-in air conditioner in the summer. I should thank her, but I doubt she lived much longer. Old ladies aren't built for car wrecks. You have to die of something and while the trauma was minor, she probably contracted pneumonia in the hospital.

The car was loud for other reasons, too. They built them loud in the '70s, I guess. That was back when gas was free and egos were growing up to be ready for the '80s.

Between the air coming in, the engine and road noise, and

the rattle of every body panel and trim piece that was about to fall off, you had to listen to music or have a conversation to stay sane.

"Did we just lose a rear quarter panel?"

I could tell by the end of our trip I was either going to love Greg or hate him, and I didn't really care which. I don't think he felt the same way because that's not really how his brain works, but it was probably still true. He just didn't realize it. If you spend enough time with someone and are actually paying attention, this is inevitable. I don't mean to give anything away, but now, several years later, I've only talked to him a couple times since pulling back into town. And it's not because I ended up hating him. I'm notorious for letting friendships fade when they're not on my mind. Greg was just what I needed at the time. I think he could have survived without me, but maybe our relationship wasn't entirely one-sided. I'd like to think I wasn't just using him as a motivator to take the trip I'd been needing.

Since we didn't have a destination, time line, or really any kind of goal in our heads, the only immediate priority was to get out of Dallas so our friends and families could carry on and realize that we were serious about going. We pulled out of Dallas and promptly pulled into Salem.

Interstate-5 will take you anywhere in the world.

We both had a different romantic idea of what a great adventure should look like - no doubt based on the books we'd read more than what we actually wanted out of life. Greg was a smooth talker and I began to think that he was merely out for more material to make himself interesting. He talked about hiking and kayaking and sleeping on the couches of people he'd just met. Are there really people like this? I had to keep reminding myself that getting out of my comfort zone was the point, so if Greg was driving me crazy by being too much of a go-getter, maybe it was a good thing and maybe I could learn something.

I had a roommate once who I came to resent because he always wanted to do what he wanted to do and I was always expected to come along and be equally excited. He wasn't doing anything wrong, but it was convenient to think so. I was raised to believe that it's offensive to disagree with someone. It became natural for me to pretend to like everything that everyone said and then I blamed them for not reading my mind when I didn't really want to go to this concert or watch that movie. If I learned anything on the road with Greg, it was to answer the question, "what do you want to do?"

In Salem we stopped at Greg's friend Josh's house to drop off a book Greg had borrowed. I wondered to myself if this whole trip was a scam. If Greg just needed someone to drive him around the country to run errands. It didn't turn out like that. I'm too sensitive sometimes.

Josh offered us a beer and some advice we didn't ask for. Something about carrying copies of our IDs because cops in Texas are so corrupt that they'll steal your wallet before asking for proof of citizenship. I think he saw it on a made-for-TV movie. Some people think the world is out to get them. I wonder how self absorbed you'd have to be to think that everyone cares enough about you to always be trying to ruin your life just for the sake of ruining it. I guess no one cared that much about Greg and I because we were generally left alone.

We thanked Josh and got in the car. The conversation from Dallas to Salem had never gotten any further than what we thought our families would do without us, so we still hadn't figured out which general direction to aim. We pulled around the corner out of sight of Josh's place and stopped the car. He was the type of guy who would have involved himself in our situation if we'd sat in his driveway for a few minutes talking about what to do.

"I've been to Seattle. Too many people up there and none of them have any appreciation for adventure." Greg was suggesting we don't go North.

I'd talked to a guy from Seattle once who told me that "the reason everyone in Seattle has money is that they all work their asses off all winter because there's nothing else to do." I wasn't interested in spending any time in a city where there's nothing better to do than work. Neither of us saw any point in going to Portland, either, since we'd taken day trips there a hundred times.

I don't remember who's idea it was, but one of us suggested that we pick two highways and flip a coin. I think there's a song about that. For now, it seemed like the best way to randomize our route. I pulled a nickle out of the ashtray and it was between I-5 North and I-5 South. I've heard it said that if you ever have a hard time choosing between two options, you should flip a coin, not because it will choose for you, but because when the coin is in the air, you'll realize which side you're hoping it lands on. We both secretly wanted I-5 Southbound. California was much more appealing than Washington. Had we just picked a route, things would have turned out much differently, but the coin picked

Northbound towards Portland, Seattle, and more of the same wet, green climate that we were trying to get away from. Don't get me wrong - we loved the Pacific Northwest. Everyone knows it's the most beautiful place on earth, but our adventure required that we get away from what was familiar.

We weren't disappointed by what fate decided. There was nothing in any direction that needed to happen. I resolved that I would take whatever I could get and enjoy the ride and I think he had the same idea. Anyway, we would have to head East eventually because he didn't have a passport to get through the border of Canada or Mexico.

I guess it was assumed that I would drive first since it was my car. We filled up at the last gas station on the way out of Salem and just caught the tail end of mid-morning traffic coming into Portland. It was raining, so everyone was driving extra fast and recklessly. It's funny how proud people get for "knowing how to drive in the rain." Every state's population thinks they have the best drivers and that every adjacent state is a death trap of uneducated dirt bags who never learned how to operate a motor vehicle. I've never understood how people can tell everything about someone else by how they drive.

"Nice blinker, asshole! Go back to California!"

A reader board told us there was a wreck further up I-5 and to expect delays. We took this as a sign that we should get onto the 84 East and skip Washington altogether. Apparently it was a good move because after about half an hour of tearing East toward the Gorge, the rain let up and the water stopped coming in through the spaces between the body and the doors.

Greg had tried plugging the gap on his side with some fast food napkins he'd found in the glove box, but rather than fixing the problem, they soaked up water and created a stream that ran down onto his leg long after the rain stopped. I was used to driving Dave in Oregon weather and didn't bother with the water coming in.

Later on, coming through Idaho, we would have the ingenious idea of gluing some strips of rubber alongside the original weatherstripping that ran around the front doors. It all but fixed the water and wind problem.

The further we got away from Dallas, and that bar, and those dead-end jobs, the more at ease I felt. For a minute I regretted that we didn't make Washington just because it was difficult to feel free while we were in our home state. Still, I knew we'd be in Idaho soon and was content to look forward to something new.

As ugly as Dave was, he wasn't gutless and I think we averaged about 80 miles per hour for the first couple of hours. I knew in the back of my mind that he wasn't going to make the whole trip, so I didn't bother driving my granny car like a granny.

four

By the time we had to stop for gas, I had started to get my head wrapped around Greg a little better. I was okay with what we were off on, but I don't know why he had decided on me as a travel partner. Maybe he was just following through on a promise he made while he was drunk. Someone did say once to "do sober what you said you'd do drunk. It will teach you to keep your mouth shut." Or something like that. I think it was Mark Twain...or maybe Hemingway. Most of the greats were drunks.

It could have just been that I was the only person he could find who was crazy enough and had a reliable enough vehicle. Whatever it was, we were stuck with each other now and I was okay with it. He seemed to be content as well, but then, he was the type to enjoy madness.

Greg had unpredictable interests. There was no rhyme or reason to which things he liked and didn't like and eventually I would give up trying to guess. As an example, he was very much a foodie and gave long lectures on the righteousness of lamb slow cooked with carrots and garlic, or mushrooms stuffed with bacon and Havarti, or whatever. Once, when I thought I had a grasp on his taste, I found myself offending him with talk of salmon and mashed potatoes. He was also a musician - which might explain the former - and didn't like other musicians unless they had succeeded in the ways of which he approved. In fact, he only really liked people who were just similar enough to him that they would agree with his ideologies, but different enough for him not to realize it. Maybe everyone is like this to an extent, but some have a wider range of tolerance for opinions that they don't agree with. When he decided he didn't like someone, that was it. I've heard that the Irish are very loyal and whether they decide to love you or hate you, they'll carry that position to the grave. Greg was probably too smart for his own good and I've heard it said that smart people are rarely happy and vice versa. Not that he wasn't happy. He just wasn't blissfully ignorant. Or ignorantly blissful. Whatever.

He also really didn't like to see people run. I don't know what it said about him, but the most irritated I ever saw him on our trip was when some fat man was having a miniature emergency outside of a gas station and running around in circles like a fool. Most people love emergencies. Try faking a heart attack in a crowded restaurant some time and you'll meet 30 patrons who are either a nurse, a firefighter, or took a first aid class in high school. Greg wasn't like most and preferred that people deal with their emergencies privately.

I don't write any of this to speak negatively about Greg, but rather to offer insight as to why things happened the way they did. I've always believed there are "types" of people. It's an unpopular opinion that sometimes gets me in trouble, but it does give the world some sense of order. Greg had a type, although maybe not like any type you've ever met. He wasn't a role model, but we had a good time over the next few weeks.

If I have a gift, it's that I can adapt to the personality of whoever I'm around. I'm sure there's a word for it. Probably just means I'm submissive. Whatever it is, it makes me easy to get along with and I find that folks who just want to be agreed with often gravitate towards me. As I've said, I tend not to disagree outwardly on issues I deem unimportant.

We hadn't said much because nothing about our surroundings was foreign enough yet to interest us. I tried to do my part by keeping my thoughts to myself. Something about how I was raised taught me that if there's one thing you don't want to be, it's annoying. Completely irrational, I know, but this is my crutch. I think it's because I was too thoughtful as a child and looked for the deeper meaning in every "go play outside," and "because I said so." I came to believe that most of the time it was a sort of shooing away I'd earned by irritating the people around me.

There were a few jokes and anecdotes as we crossed Oregon and neared Idaho, but nothing with much substance. I started to wonder how Greg would react when something went wrong. I remembered him being pretty even-tempered back in school, but maybe he was the type to lose his mind when things didn't go well. I had a brief memory of how my old friend Eric had a meltdown when he dented his dad's garage door with a skateboard. I guess it would stress anyone out, but I was more the type to stand back and be fascinated by such events. My mother could tell of how I've always watched the unexpected unfold with interest more than with worry. As long as it wasn't my problem, that is. Another characteristic that got me into trouble sometimes.

~

It was afternoon when we hit a quarter of a tank and decided to stop in Baker City. The gas gauge was working that day so I wasn't as concerned about keeping the tank full as I sometimes am. We probably could have made it out of Oregon, but having our gas pumped by someone else one more time was too appealing.

There was a pretty girl behind the counter, so Greg had to go in and find something to buy. I wasn't sure if I'd ever see him again. This became the norm, and by Wyoming, I had come to expect it.

Some people have a knack for meeting folks. I could barely hold a conversation with my own friends and family, but Greg knew just what to say to make anyone love him. The irony was that once he knew someone, he rarely liked them anymore. This could be why he learned to make friends so efficiently. The sheer volume of acquaintances he made almost guaranteed he'd always have one or two friends. He wasn't particularly good-looking, but he was particularly charming. Somewhere in Arkansas after an especially successful afternoon of friend-making, I told him he should write a book.

"Ha! That would require me to believe that people should be more like me."

"You're right, Man. There are already way too many of you."

"Could you imagine if there were 5, or 10, or 100 people just like me walking the earth? The whole planet would burn down."

I didn't really know what he meant, but I don't think he really thought of himself as a role model.

Greg finally came out with two pepperoni sticks and a 6-pack of Pabst. I could see his lady-friend smiling after him through the window. If he swept her off her feet that easily, maybe I would go try my luck. A sort of social experiment, of course. I remembered that I had brought a pipe, but never got around to buying tobacco, and while gas station pipe tobacco is the worst you can get, it gave me an excuse to go in.

"Good afternoon."

"Hello." She looked bored.

"Do you guys have any pipe tobacco?"

She turned around to look over the cigarettes and, after 30 seconds of watching her peruse, I felt my question had been answered.

"Don't worry about it. Maybe just some Black & Milds." She wouldn't have been able to find those either, but I pointed and talked very slowly. "Thanks."

"Have a nice day."

Back outside, Greg was already through the first processed meat stick and onto the second. He obviously hadn't gotten two so he could share.

"Want me to drive, Man?"

"Go for it. Feel free to crash this beast." I was only half joking. That's when it hit me that I'd never been in a car with Greg driving, and, while it normally wouldn't make any difference, I was committed to hundreds or maybe thousands of miles in the passenger seat at his mercy. Of course, my worst fears were never realized and he only drove a little crazier than I. That's not hard to do as I've been told I drive like a geriatric. I did find, however, that I had to pay attention to where we were going. Greg had a terrible sense of direction and more than once, after stopping for gas or sleep, aimed our steed back in the direction from which we came. Maybe he did it on purpose since we didn't care where we ended up.

I helped myself to one of his PBRs and handed him one. "Did you know it's only a traffic infraction in Oregon to drink while driving? It's not on the same level as driving drunk although more often than not they go hand-in-hand." I wasn't positive, but I thought I had heard that somewhere.

"That blonde told me we should go to New York City. I almost convinced her to come with us."

"She would have had to sit on the roof."

five

"When did using poor English become good marketing?"

As we drove past towns and gas stations on our way East, I noticed a trend in advertizing in which a business would spell a word or two wrong in their product or company name. It seemed to be a particular problem in the coffee industry.

"I know, Dude. One nation under-educated."

"Does spelling 'Koffee' with a 'K' attract more business?" I wondered out loud. Dave seemed to demonstrate his agreement by running rougher as we passed more and more of these establishments.

It must have been a fairly new epidemic, or I just hadn't paid attention before. Now that I wasn't driving, I was able to look around.

Coming from a small town, I had spent my life surrounded by old-fashioned types who didn't catch on to trends very urgently. It must have been for this reason that I was and am a firm believer in proper syntax. My generation is notorious for taking short cuts in writing, but I've never believed the time saved was worth seeming lazy and uneducated. With the proliferation of computers has come the trend of using "U" for "you," "4" for "for," and "K" for "okay." While I've never gotten worked up about much, I do believe that there are few things more valuable than a good reputation and few things more difficult to repair than one that has been damaged or poorly built. I had a friend in high school who had to resubmit an important paper several times because he had become used to writing with deplorable grammar and and spelling and had forgotten how to write correctly when the need arose.

Greg must have shared my opinion on the whole thing because his reply was, "I never put anything in my body that's spelled wrong."

That was good enough for me and I resolved not to stop anywhere with the name "Kaffeine Krazy," or "Brad'z Burgurz." While it made sustenance harder to find, I felt better knowing that we were only supporting professionals and that by selling one less product, those who had flunked out of 3rd grade would be forced to shut down and go back to school.

We were within sight of the Idaho border and Greg was standing on the gas pedal more furiously the closer we got. I think the beers helped. It seemed like no one else in the world was on their way from Oregon to Idaho that evening and we could really move not having to deal with traffic. I wondered if truck drivers were scam artists just moving the same products back and forth so they'd always have a job.

Greg took us over the line out of our home state and we were free. I'd flown to other states and countries before, but in a plane, you never know when you're crossing a border. Even driving to Washington as we both had a hundred times was nothing like tearing East across the country and making the first milestone. Passing the "Welcome to Idaho" sign was more than a physical border. We had crossed a psychological boundary and it truly felt like we were on our way.

six

Now that any remaining sense of urgency had evaporated, we cruised more slowly for the next couple hours. I watched the cars around us and played games in my head. Whenever we drove under an overpass where another car was passing over, I would use a sailor trick to figure out if we would crash had we been on the same plane. I went sailing with a man named Gerald once and he taught me a trick where one could look past another boat to a point on the horizon and if the other boat's position in relation to the point didn't change as you sailed along, you were on course to run into each other. If that makes any sense.

When I was a child, I couldn't understand how all of the cars kept from running into each other. To an untrained observer, traffic looks terribly random. Controlled chaos. Of course, it really is random in places like Kampala.

We pulled into a town called Glenns Ferry when Greg got tired of driving. It's amazing how the whole world becomes your campsite when you aren't high-maintenance. Not having a tent or a trailer, we could really stop and lean the seats back in any parking lot or rest stop.

Since it was our first night, we were a little picky about where we would sleep, but we would realize quickly that anywhere the car could come to a stop was good enough. We finally decided on a side parking lot next to the grocery store downtown. No one bothered us there and we would have slept wonderfully if the seats had folded down like we planned. I'd never tried to sleep in Dave before and we were both surprised to find that neither seat would comply. The handle to lean the driver's seat back was broken off and the passenger's seat never had the option.

Greg made the mistake of telling me that he could sleep anywhere, so I let him figure out a way to get comfortable in the front while I moved to the back seat. The real problem was that we weren't exhausted enough yet from the trip. There's no point in trying to sleep for your first couple nights on the road. After about a week, you'll fall asleep any time your eyes shut whether you want to or not.

~

It's always interested me to read the biographies of legends and learn of the exact moment when, say, Steinbeck became successful. He was probably bursting with potential long before he ever did anything worthwhile, but nobody would give him a chance until he proved himself. I guess the same thing happened to the Beatles. Apparently in the talent realm, one is guilty until proven innocent. Makes you wonder how many of the folks who you run into would have been famous if their circumstances were different. Had they just been born in a different location, or ever tried putting a paintbrush to canvas. Perhaps fame is entirely the result of properly directed motivation. Not that being a celebrity is worth anything.

Maybe Einstein was right when he said that everyone's a genius. Of course it's been pointed out that if everybody is, then no one is. By definition, half of the people you run into will be of below average intelligence. But that doesn't bother me as much as the fact that half the cars on the road are controlled by below average drivers. This actually has the potential to affect me directly on a road trip. My cousin drives an ambulance in rural Missouri and tells horror stories about the car wrecks he's seen. There's a job I couldn't do.

It seemed like I'd read somewhere that car accidents are the leading cause of death among people my age and I considered this fact over a cup of coffee. After our first night sleeping in Dave, we found a diner in Glenns Ferry and ordered the "cup of mud." I never did figure out if it was a clever name for coffee or if I'd actually been served mud. At least it was spelled correctly.

I only drink coffee when people are watching. It's easier than explaining that I don't like it. I've been told I should be more assertive, but when I have an unpopular opinion, it's often simpler to follow the crowd, especially when it really doesn't matter. There are some conversations that aren't worth having on a regular basis. The concept of acquired taste doesn't make any sense to me. You force yourself to partake of something that you don't like until your body gives in and starts enjoying it - often to the point of developing a dependency. Ironically, it's usually something that will kill you. I am guilty of liking beer, so I guess I've cooperated.

Greg was reading a three day old paper and I was transferring ice cubes from my water to my coffee. It wasn't too hot - I was just seeing how high I could raise the beverage without it spilling over. Greg noticed what I was doing and kicked the table to be funny. The waitress was not amused by the mess that resulted. I called him an asshole and resolved to tip her an extra dollar to make up for the mud puddle.

"I think we should stay out of the big cities. They're all the same." He already regretted spilling my coffee and was trying to change the subject. I didn't care as much as I pretended to because I didn't want to drink it anyway.

"What do you think the world was like before chain stores? Imagine every new place you went having all new businesses. Nothing was based on a big box formula. I bet grocery stores felt more honest and raw. The guy behind the counter was just a guy - not part of a multinational machine." I really wasn't alluding to any kind of political bent. "Hell, you could probably drive to the next town up the road and find a restaurant serving food that you'd never heard of." I was feeling a little jealous of people 50 years ago who could drive for a couple hours and be in a place where nothing resembled anything else. It seems like, more and more, everything is just this place's version of that place's...thing. From music, to fashion, to commerce. Could it be a coincidence that every major truck company makes a vehicle that's basically the same as what the others make? Even though they would say so in court, I don't believe that each of them came up with their design independently. Then again, the telephone was invented by two guys at once who didn't know each other. Bell just got his patent letter in first and only by several hours.

"I don't know, Dude. No one really knew that they had it good back then, so it wasn't as ideal as you'd think. And they had it worse than us in other ways. Given the option, they probably would have preferred to live in our world with all the conveniences. There really were no good old days." Greg liked to look at the opposite side of things. I agreed with him, but I thought he was missing my point.

"Well, should we flip a coin again, or do you have a preference? I think we're almost to the I-86, I-84 split."

"Let's just get to Utah and away from the rain." It had been raining as long as we'd been in Idaho and Greg was hoping for a change of scenery. "I don't care what happens after that."

It was 11:00 by the time we paid for breakfast and got back to the car. The waitress looked glad to see us go. It was the only emotion I'd seen her show since we came in. Thinking back on it, she was probably disgusted that we'd brushed our teeth and changed clothes in her bathroom. Most of the folks we met on our trip either thought we were nasty hobos or exciting adventurers. Neither of us had slept well and apparently Greg wasn't up for laying on the charm. I would soon came to appreciate where his smooth talking got us and how it would bring us favor with the locals wherever we went. As much as I sometimes felt he was a bit of a schmooze, I was glad to be on his side.

I went for the driver's seat and Greg didn't argue. We fueled up before pushing East and discussed how to make sleeping more comfortable. I almost volunteered to sleep in the trunk, but I thought he would take me seriously.

As we passed Twin Falls, Idaho, I wondered if every state has a Twin Falls. Oregon does, I thought, or maybe that was Twin Rocks. Maybe if someone fell off the rocks they'd change the name. Doesn't every state have a Springfield? I know that there's a Las Vegas in New Mexico, and a Nevada, Missouri. Missouri is awfully confused, really. More of Kansas City is located in Missouri than in Kansas. Maybe the first inhabitants of the Kansas town thought it would be ironic to build East.

I was distracted by rambling thoughts when we made the split and I accidentally hit 86 North toward the 15. You have to take an exit to stay on 84 and when we realized my mistake, we had to backtrack for twenty minutes. It didn't bother us much, but we had made the mistake of having a tentative plan and it always messes with your stomach to screw up the plan.

We were back on track and hit Utah in an hour. Dave was cranky about the high altitude, but our conversation had turned to books, so we weren't paying much attention to the ride. I'd never been much a reader of fiction and Greg was trying to cure me of that. Years later, I have him to thank for turning me onto folks like Bukowski and Marquez. A little cliche, maybe, but they're Greats for a reason. Now I recommend "One Hundred Years of Solitude" to everyone I know.

If I have one regret in life, it's that I didn't start reading fiction earlier.

Our discussion wandered like the road from books to movies to current events to a word or two on religion. It was nice to talk to someone about the things that go on in my head. Greg was a thinker, but you wouldn't have known without spending some time with him.

For a while, we talked about the idea of probability as it applies to risk. My position was that if we really understood the chances of, say, dying in a wreck, would it affect our decision to drive? Would going to the grocery store for a snack be worth risking death? I don't know if I buy the whole idea. I'm not saying the math is bad, I just think there must be more to it. If the odds of crashing your car for a bag of chips was one in a thousand, or even one in a million, then by going, you'd have to admit that getting the chips is worth dying. Greg agreed, but offered that probability isn't really the chances of something happening, it's just how many times there will be a certain outcome for the number of total attempts. That made more sense to me because I was unwilling to admit that going to work was worth dying on the way. He set me at ease with the promise that stupid people make up most of the negative outcomes. Maybe I'm fooling myself, but whenever I get in the car, I know I'm going to make it to my destination.

When the conversation stalled for more than a few minutes, Greg picked up the old newspaper he had stolen from the diner. I had a friend years ago who told me that her Grandma could read the same newspaper several times a day and always be captivated by the stories. That's the beauty of Alzheimer's, I guess. Greg was just a slow reader. I think he liked to squeeze every bit of substance from each article. That's probably why he always knew what was going on in the world.

"Look at the used car ads when you get a chance."

"Ha! Are you trying to jinx us?"

"It's not for me...it's for my sister. She needs a car," I lied. He knew I was lying, too. Who would buy a car 800 miles away? It wasn't a very well thought out story.

"Good, because we can't afford one."

"How do you know? Did you count the money?" I was happy to put the focus off of myself and onto him. Greg just smiled and kept reading about the war in Iraq.

The signs and the traffic were starting to tell us that we were nearing Salt Lake City. Dave never did too well in stop and go traffic. I've heard that old Volkswagens are air-cooled and you have to keep moving at top speed just to stop the motor from overheating and dropping out from under you. Dave wasn't quite that temperamental, but it was time to make a choice before the highway chose for us.

Again we flipped our nickel and it told us to take I-80 and scream across Wyoming. I'd never checked Dave's top speed, but I knew we'd probably find out today.

One of the great attractions of Wyoming is that the highways are red from the local rock used in the concrete. It also creates a different brand of road noise that I found more pleasant than the highways in Utah and Idaho.

In Lyman, we stopped for gas and discussed sleeping there or pressing on. I was tired of driving and Greg was tired of reading old news. We'd both brought reading material, but, of course, it was still in the trunk.

We weren't used to pumping our own gas yet and we sat in the car for a few minutes before realizing that no one was coming to do it for us. Greg got out to pump and I went to find a bathroom. I chose the only stall with a door and stayed in there longer than necessary reading the graffiti. The grammar was more fascinating than the content.

"TYLer IS gAAY"

You don't want to be gay in rural Wyoming. Or maybe Tyler was the author and took advantage of the the only stall with a door to come out anonymously. I hoped Tyler had a good life.

On my way back to the car, I noticed that there was already a puddle of oil building under the engine. Dave had a terrible oil habit and I'd been meaning to have an intervention. Today it was looking like something had really come loose, so I turned around to go pay $7.00 for minute mart oil. Since I was feeding Dave, I thought I deserved a snack, too, and bought some off-brand chips with a boring picture on the bag. I judge food by its label, but Dave and I couldn't both have the good stuff. They were probably more healthy than the expensive bag anyway.

Greg was talking to an ugly brunette when I returned. Something about how she had family in Portland and maybe we knew them. He was humoring her and I stayed out of it. After adding the quart of oil, I got in the passenger seat and daydreamed about living on a sailboat.

seven

I've never wanted to be a hippy, but probably only because it's a title. I probably didn't want to be anything that people considered me to be. As long as I didn't know what category I fit into, I was okay with it. Really, I just didn't want to be naked in public or do drugs which is what I thought hippies did. Later on I would realize that it's more of a blanket term used for wanderers, people who drive certain cars, people with long hair, people who wear certain kinds of clothes, don't wear shoes, vote a certain way, don't like to work, etc. It used to really mean something, but I think our generation can't or doesn't want to come up with a new take on life so we just borrow from generations before us. Some people would argue that that IS our lifestyle - taking what we like about other worldviews and making our own.

Well, I guess every generation has done that since the beginning of time. Maybe what defines a generation is really just a combination of the current politics, technology, and events. Even the hippies had to base their views on something. And it happened to come out of war. It's ironic that the flower generation owes who they were to war - not to peace. An era of peace would have given them entirely different things to fight for and sing about. Maybe the reason that our parents' generation was so loud and naughty in the 80s was that they grew up in times of peace and were looking for conflict. The government wouldn't give them war, so they made their own war with big hair and loud music and loud clothes and loud cars and yelling and drinking and fighting and smashing guitars.

Humans have been at war for thousands of years and the only thing peace has ever given us was enough idleness to get annoyed at each other and start a fight and enough prosperity to fund it.

I wonder what will drive future generations to do what they

will do. And I wonder if geography still affects how people turn out in a world that is getting smaller. Eventually we will all know the same things because we'll all read the same news and work for the same companies and drive the same floating cars. Maybe someday there will only be one worldview because all of the same facts will be available to everyone. The only difference between people will be what they believe that can't be proven and which things are more important than others.

I think if Huxley turns out to be right, it won't be because anyone had malevolent intentions, but because efficiency and security and entertainment have become higher priorities than anything else and social norms naturally adjust to compensate. In my opinion, where he's wrong is in thinking that the government has to manipulate the population into wanting certain things and letting others go unnoticed. Politicians aren't that smart. I would suggest that he's close, but, really, the population already wants the most fun with the least effort and the government is changing to accommodate - not the other way around. When folks get up in arms about the government taking away our guns - or whatever - I can't help but think that Washington only has as much power as it is given by the voters. Every congressman who sponsors a bill, popular or not, was put into office by a majority of voters. And probably 100% of the time, the bill doesn't force anything on the people that they don't already believe in, even if they don't realize they believe in it. As an example, the folks who want to see less police involvement and an overall smaller government are the same people who want every criminal pursued tirelessly until they're brought to justice and locked up for life. Perhaps a better example would be those who see corruption on a national level and call for action while boldly wearing their own local brand of corruption in the form of a police or firefighter sticker on the back of their car that essentially says, "don't give me a ticket...I'm one of you." I can't say how many times I've been in the car with an overzealous friend or family member who decried the lack of police around when someone in another car rolled a stop sign, but, needless to say, they weren't happy to see an officer when they were the one caught speeding or driving drunk. A man named Bill Vaughan said that "a true patriot is the fellow who gets a parking ticket and rejoices that the system works."

I know a guy who thinks that we should turn the Middle East into a sheet of glass, presumably because they don't do things our way. Ironically, that's exactly the opinion of the minority over there who is causing problems - to kill everyone who doesn't agree with them. So, my friend believes the same thing that he would have them die for believing. If terrorism could be defined as believing that others should die for not holding your opinions, I have bad news for a lot of Americans.

Sometimes I read the news and am glad to see that things are falling apart. It gives me hope that people will start doing the right thing if they realize that the deterioration of what they love can be directly attributed to their own actions. But, I guess no one ever considers that they could be the problem. You can talk to a hundred people - even corrupt, incompetent people - and each one will have the opinion that he is good at his job but is surrounded by idiots. Every broken relationship will have two victims, neither of which will ever admit to doing anything wrong other than trusting the other. Even the bad guys always think that they're doing the right thing. If they didn't, they would change sides. Likewise, all of this is only what makes sense to me and my worldview and if you found someone who disagreed (which is the simplest thing of all) he would have just as logical of an argument for why I'm more incompetent than those who I find to be the problem.

Some people believe that all humans are inherently evil but can be good sometimes. Others believe that we're essentially good, but make poor decisions when selfishness takes over. I don't know which view I subscribe to and I don't know what my point is.

On a lighter note, it's interesting to consider that people cross paths en route to each others' home state or country for vacation. If a guy who lives in Montana drives Southeast and passes the guy driving Northwest from Florida, maybe they should have just stayed home and enjoyed the beauty and adventure of home. If two guys pass each other on the way to work every day, maybe they should just trade jobs and both benefit from working closer to home. I know there's more to it than that. Soon, we'll all be able to work from the couch and order our groceries delivered and never leave the house. I wonder what effect maximum efficiency will have on the population. Did the laborers who connected the country with railroad tracks realize that they were benefiting more from getting out and working with their hands than the sum of their work benefited the company or the country. Somewhere along the line people came to think that work was more of a necessary evil than it was a blessing to the worker. Ironically, folks will dodge heavy lifting while at their place of employment then pay for the use of a gym where they can work and sweat for hours while producing nothing.

On the subject of moving from one place to another, maybe the fat, hairy, dirty old men who ride the bus in circles all day aren't as crazy as the rest of the riders believe. They may be getting as much or more done than the people with somewhere to be and everyone ends up back where they started anyway.

Some people go to work so they can pay for a car to get to work.

Debt uses the same logic, but is more subtle. One must borrow money in order to have a better credit score so that one may borrow more money and increase ones credit score to borrow more money to develop more credit and so forth.

And one must work at a job to gain experience so that one may get a job that requires experience and then gain experience in order to get a job. I've heard people say hundreds of times that "it will look good on a resume," but I've never figured out why it is so important to have an excellent resume rather than an excellent job or even a job one enjoys.

Somehow the goal has become to die with a fabulous resume and an impeccable credit score.

eight

I must have fallen asleep because I was awoken by a terrible noise coming from the other side of the firewall. It was dark outside and Greg was driving about 100 with the headlights off. An interesting tactic, but I couldn't see any reason to argue.

"What the hell is that?" I yelled over the din.

"Well, the good news is that I think this old Ford will get us as far as Cheyenne."

"Did you run over a lawnmower? And why are the headlights off?" It seemed like a good time to pose the question. I was confused and bothered by everything. Where were we? What was happening to the car? Had I slept through anything important? Why wasn't Greg in a mental hospital?

"I'm driving by moonlight. It's how Lewis and Clark did it."

"Pull over, Man. I'm not going down with this ship." As much as I didn't want to be stranded in the desert, I had heard stories of cars with shattered suspension components assuming steering control and taking sweet old couples right off the road and into the afterlife. Actually, if that was the problem, Dave would have been repairable and could have gotten us a couple states further along. I was in denial, though, and I knew in the back of my mind that Henry Ford was about to leave us stranded with the most expensive of car troubles. It's amazing how fixing a car can cost more than the car is worth. I had a fleeting thought about starting a business in which I would buy a car and quadruple my money by tearing it down and selling the parts. It's probably been done before. I guess the labor is what gets you.

"It's nothing, Bro. We passed a semi two hours ago that was completely flipped over onto its side. That guy had it bad. Spilled his chickens all over the road."

"Uh...just because someone else has it worse doesn't mean we don't have it bad." I remembered what my parents used to say about starving children in Africa. As if I could solve the problem by finishing my kale.

I felt like I was not in control of the situation and it made me anxious. I was supposed to be the cool one. Greg was charming and clinically insane, but I was the level-headed one who would keep us out of trouble.

"Relax, Dude. What could possibly go wrong? You didn't think this car would take us all the way to Spain, did you? Let's at least get to the next town and sleep for the night. In the morning, we can either fix the problem or drop a match in the gas tank."

I was oddly okay with his solution, but no sooner had I resolved to let the adventure have me than the most terrible sound yet crunched and squeaked and popped out at us and Dave breathed his last breath.

"JUHJUHJUH...juh...juh...gah..........gah............brbrbbrbrrb brbrbrbrrrrrr............uuuuuurrrrrrrggggggggggaaaaaahhhhhhhhhhhhhh hhhhhhh...," Dave stated very matter-of-factly.

"Whatever. You're buying the next car," I mumbled in Greg's general direction.

"Hey, asshole, I just happened to be driving this pile when it died." He coasted far off the road onto the dirt shoulder and pushed hard on the brakes to bring the late Dave to a thumping stop.

Greg enjoys confrontation. He says it's the only way to get things done. He also says that if things aren't stirred up once in a while, people become stagnant. I learned at an early age not to talk about issues. The shit stirred up and the hurt feelings are always worse than the problem one is trying to address. I alienated a few friends this way before I figured out that I was the problem. You really can't be more concerned about someone's character than they are.

I used to know a guy who believed very strongly in his decision not to shave his beard because Jesus Christ had a beard. I guess he thought it gave him some kind of a moral edge to adopt the same policy as the Messiah. Last I heard, he is okay with dodging taxes, stealing from his employer, and cheating on his girlfriend, but still thinks that God is very proud of him for not wavering on the facial hair subject. I guess people prefer to believe whatever is most convenient. The caveat to intellectual honesty is that if someone is bright enough to see the value in it, they're also clever enough to justify anything that they want to do.

Confrontation is only worthwhile if you come out ahead.

Maybe Greg's just better at it than I am. Or maybe he enjoys being at odds. Even when I win an argument using logic, I feel I have lost because I've only succeeded in showing someone else that they're wrong. It's probably more noble to let everyone think what they want to think. I find more and more that the less I say, the simpler my world becomes.

Neither of us were actually mad. If we weren't so stubborn, we'd have realized that the breakdown was much more conducive to adventure than if the Ford had survived. Actually, Greg seemed entirely okay with the whole thing. I think he was more reacting to my outburst than to our situation. Funny how I'd left Dallas with the expectation that Dave wouldn't be coming home with me, but now that I wasn't in charge of my circumstances, it didn't seem like such a romantic idea. On the plus side, Dave's untimely death had the immediate effect of ripping me from my comfort zone and throwing me into a series of events that I would never have allowed to happen if I'd had a car that ran or enough money to acquire one.

It didn't seem to be worth popping the hood in the dark, so we assumed the positions and tried to sleep. Wyoming is a cold place in February and we didn't have the luxury of starting the car every couple hours just to run the heater.

"You know, cuddling is really the best way to keep warm while slee-"

"Ha!" I didn't let him finish. "Not unless I can put a bag over your head."

~

In the morning we popped the hood and pretended to know what we were looking at. The only thing I knew how to do was check the oil, so I pulled the dipstick and found it dry. Dave's addiction had been his demise.

"I think that's the problem."

"You're like a wise old sage," I grinned and poked Greg in the ribs.

We bummed around on the side of the road for a while and mulled over what we should do.

"We could just settle in right here. Build ourselves a nice hut. Maybe set up a gas station." It was the best idea I could come up with. "How far do you think we are from Laramie?" I was looking at the old atlas we'd brought along. "If we get there we could probably sell the car and get a bus to Cheyenne." I hadn't planned any further than that, but for whatever reason, I thought that getting to Cheyenne would solve all our problems. Not that we had any problems.

Greg lit a cigarette and didn't answer.

"I didn't know you smoked."

"I don't. This seems like a good time to start." I could tell he hated it.

"You know, cigarettes are one of the leading causes of statistics."

"Don't judge me."

"How far do you think you drove last night after we got gas?"

"The last sign I saw said Laramie was 20 miles away." He was trying to stack round rocks on top of each other like you see in photos of Utah. "Hey!" It sounded like he had an idea. "My mom broke down driving a minivan through Wyoming a few years ago."

"A true family tradition. Shall we walk and talk?" Greg gave up on his rock pile and joined me walking East. "With any luck, someone will steal the car and all our worldly possessions." I racked my brain for anything I should have grabbed out of the trunk. None of it seemed important. Just as I suspected, we hadn't used anything we'd brought along.

After a few miles and some laughs to distract us, the pain in my feet gave me enough courage to stick a thumb out. In the movies when you hitchhike, the first car that comes along always picks you up. I learned after some more miles that I'm living in the wrong era. A few roadside murderers have ruined hitchhiking for everyone as usually happens. My Dad told me before we left that I should have gotten a AAA membership (a AAA...an AAA...or is it Triple A?). I agreed and never followed through. I guess it wouldn't have helped since we still would have had to walk to a phone to call the 1-800 number. If you can't get someone to stop and pick you up, you'd have as much luck borrowing a cell phone from the guy passing you at 85 miles per hour.

Greg suggested I lay in the road. That would get someone to stop. And if it didn't, at least I wouldn't have to worry about getting a ride anymore.

"I would pick us up. We seem like a couple of wholesome guys."

"Maybe if we had some face tattoos," Greg offered.

"Teardrop tattoos under our eyes? I have a felt pen..."

"I guess if anything, we should look more pitiful and helpless." It was his turn to be the voice of reason. "I think the key is traveling with a pet. Could you walk on all fours?"

I thought of the commercials on TV imploring you to sponsor a child. Some college did a study comparing heart-wrenching commercials. Apparently people are more likely to donate when they see sad puppies than sad children.

"Well, if we have to walk any further, I'm going to be crawling on my hands and knees whether I want to or not."

We saw the big green exit sign for Laramie just as I was starting to consider joining the marines. They would probably be happy to come pick me up in exchange for 4 years of service to Washington and the good ol' boys running things. At least getting blown up in Wherever-stan would be a more honorable death than being eaten by tumbleweed, or wild boar, or whatever kills folks in the Midwest. I wondered if my family back home would miss me or if they'd be more proud that they'd told me so. If I died on the road they would know they had been right about the world and would always tell the story of their son/brother/cousin who left home and was murdered, that's right, murdered by the hostile natives of Wyoming.

"It's dangerous out there. I hear they hate Northwesterners. Don't let 'em see your license plate or they'll drive by and shoot you dead while you sleep in your car. Yep, the further East you go, the more uncivilized people are. Even the locals just about can't walk through their own neighborhood. Children get shot every day in the suburbs of Milwaukee. Right in their front yard."

Just as I dropped my thumb for the last time, a late model pickup pulled off up ahead of us and a 50-something professional type stepped out.

"Are you two trying to get to Cheyenne?"

"Nah, we're stopping here in Laramie," Greg beat me to it. "Thanks, though. Where were you three hours ago?"

"That must be your Oldsmobile a few miles back." We didn't bother correcting him.

I stepped in. "Are you from here?" I wasn't sure where "here" was. "We're going to Cheyenne eventually. Anything worth seeing when we get there?"

"I'm from further West, but I always stop at the Redwood on Lincoln whenever I make it out there. Cheap beers at that place. Good luck, fellas." He'd done his good deed by stopping and didn't seem to want to chit-chat.

We walked the rest of the way into town and found Wyoming's version of a coffee shop. As one would expect, it was wildly different from an Oregon coffee shop. The people in middle America didn't seem to be motivated by what others thought was cool. Most exciting to me was that I had non-coffee options to choose from. A guy was liable to be laughed out of town for requesting a drink void of espresso within 100 miles of Portland. I ordered a Coke and sat down at the customer computer. Greg was looking over a shelf of romance novels. Apparently whoever ran the place thought that having a collection of books was more important than what the books are about.

A quick internet search uncovered a local yard that would come pick up your car and give you cash. It sounded too good to be true and I didn't get my hopes up. Fixing the car was never an option in my mind. I could have probably bought a Ferrari for cheaper than getting Dave towed and having the work done. Greg had a knack for keeping occupied, but not by doing anything productive. By the time I'd pieced together a plan, he had won over the barista, beat himself in chess, and discussed German history with a semi-oblivious University of Wyoming student named Adam. Nice kid, but he needed to get out more. Don't we all? He was some kind of arts major. I don't remember in what, but surely he'd never use his degree if he ever finished getting it. College is entirely a social endeavor anyway. It hasn't been about education since probably the '80s.

"Hey, make yourself useful and call this scrap yard," I offered Greg a way to help. "Do you know anything about this place, Adam?"

"I don't live here...I just come for the coffee." I didn't believe him.

"It's your car, Dude." Greg grinned. I knew he was willing to help, but wasn't in as much of a hurry as I was.

"You broke it," I mumbled. Adam loaned me his cell phone and I made the call.

Some years ago in some third-world country I learned to haggle. It's not the same as arguing, so I'm not opposed. Or maybe the potential to save money overrides my tendency to avoid confrontation. I knew we wouldn't get much for Dave. The condition I really wanted added to the deal was a ride to and from the roadside spot where he died. The call-taker, who was also the driver, agreed to take me out there but, as I expected, he would pay less than the gas in the Ford's tank was worth. The problem with dealing with a junk yard is that they always have the upper hand. For all they cared, we could leave Dave on the side of I-80 forever. We never would have gotten our bags back that way, so I told him where to pick me up since Greg and Adam didn't look like they were going anywhere anytime soon.

I never asked the tow-truck driver his name, but he looked exactly like every tow-truck driver, so I'll spare you the description. It was amazing how quickly we did the several miles that it had taken Greg and and I hours to walk. I was glad Dave was still there as I'm sure what's-his-name would have left me on the side of the road for lying about a car that didn't exist. I wasn't taking that walk again, but maybe our well-dressed friend from that afternoon would have picked me up on his way back West and I could have hitchhiked to Albuquerque or San Diego.

It was getting dark and I wondered if the coffee shop would still be open. I hadn't made plans on where to meet Greg when I got back. My chauffeur had Dave hooked up surprisingly quickly and made some joke about how we should have just driven the car straight to the junkyard. I could tell he said the same thing to every customer. On the way back, I wondered if he'd actually pay me or maybe just kick me out. He obviously wasn't a bad guy, but I was feeling exposed by the whole thing and forgot that people are generally more helpful than malicious.

To break the silence, he lectured a little on the nature of small towns as we drove. "Ya know, there's nowhere to go in this country...folks move away from the city to get away from it all and here come some more folks who want the same thing and, before you know it, the place is full up with fast food joints and shoppin' malls to feed and clothe everybody who wanted to get away from the burger shops and malls. The dern thing just turns into a city! Where can a guy go? Doesn't Walmart realize that some towns don't want 'em?," and so forth. The more worked up he got, the more I tried to agree with him in a soothing tone.

The coffee shop was closed when we made it to Laramie, but Greg and Adam had only moved 10 feet to the other side of the front door.

"So are we rich?" Greg came over to help me unload our bags before Dave rolled away to be cannibalized so old farmers could keep their daily drivers running. Actually, he probably would be crushed and melted and made into ugly furniture for rich people.

"That chair you're sitting on is made from 100% recycled American steel," they would tell their friends who would then have to go buy something more responsibly constructed and with a higher sticker price. There's a direct correlation between how expensive a piece is and how strongly it gives you the urge to leave the room. Wasn't it Picasso who said that most art is created to make rich people feel special and important? I think the art world is about 20% creativity and 80% marketing. The real task isn't making something beautiful, but convincing people that they should think it's beautiful.

I didn't care what happened to Dave, but I would probably tell my uncle that I traded him in for something nicer which I promptly totaled when a drunk driver crossed the center line. "Well, cars can be replaced. I'm just glad you're alive." It would take his mind off my irresponsible maintenance record. Senior family members love to think that their nieces/nephews/grandchildren would be ahead in life if they weren't at the mercy of all the idiots in the world.

"Adam said we can stay at his place tonight and he'll take us to Cheyenne tomorrow."

"Right on. Thanks, Man." I welcomed the idea of sleeping somewhere warm.

nine

Adam lived just West of Laramie and slightly north off some frontage road. We pulled into the driveway and it looked more normal than I thought was possible. I couldn't tell in the dark whether the acreage around the house was part of the same estate and seeing it in the light probably wouldn't have helped. The land was likely used for something in the warmer months. Or not. Whoever was in charge kept the yard up, but the inside smelled like a woman hadn't lived there in years. Maybe ever. It wasn't bad - just stale. I have a friend who got married recently and the smell of his house changed drastically the day his wife moved in.

Two other college types were planted on the couch in the first room watching some reality show marathon. I figured one of them owned the house, or his parents did, and he rented rooms to his friends from school to pay the mortgage while Mom and Dad spent the winter in Florida, or Morocco, or wherever old people go to blow money and nurse their arthritis. On the Pacific side of the Rockies, retirees migrate to Arizona. On the other side of the continental divide, folks are loyal to an entirely different selection of destinations. It doesn't make any sense to me that being a thousand miles away from your family is better than being two, or three, or ten thousand miles away. Things change when you have grandkids, I guess. Or senility kicks in. Or the couple hours saved on an emergency flight home makes miserable Arizona a superior option to Palm Springs. I refuse to believe that anybody actually likes Phoenix.

Adam's friends didn't act like it was rare to see a couple strangers in their house. The hairy one got up and introduced himself as Michael (not Mike) and his buddy as Rob. Adam brought out beers and we took our spots on the floor. Rob quickly got up and offered us the couch and I realized I'd misjudged him. I didn't mean to form an opinion within seconds of meeting them, but I'm sure I'd been conditioned by something growing up. You always hear that hate - I didn't hate anyone, but as an example - hate is learned, not inherent. I've always wondered, if that's the case, who taught the first haters to hate?

"Where are you guys from?" Michael seemed genuinely interested and Rob focused on the TV. The strong, silent type, I figured. Probably a welder. Or a mechanic. Maybe he could have fixed the car. I looked for grease stains on his hands to confirm, but found none. Probably a cattle farmer.

"Portland." I didn't know if Greg was trying to sound interesting or if this was his solution to the Dallas, Oregon dilemma. Everyone wants to be from Portland. I let him fill them in on the rest of the story. I never watched much television at home and was fascinated by what the people on the screen were willing to do for half an hour of fame. I wondered if dignity was more valuable than time. As much as I would have wanted to deny it, I probably would have been willing to look like a fool in front of a national audience for a day. If it paid well enough, of course. I decided that the reason we didn't see the same types of shows 50 years ago probably wasn't that they hadn't been conceived yet, but that people were less willing to sell their reputation. You really can't fault the contestants. It's the national viewership who wants to see people fail. Probably makes them feel better about themselves.

Then again, maybe I was over thinking it. Maybe some producer somewhere realized that you can fire all the writers and actors and make just as much money sticking a few abrasive personalities in a small space and letting them destroy each other. That's a winning formula. How must the auditions for those shows look?

"We can't stand you. When can you start?"

My friend Kate was telling me about a college class she took in which they discussed our aging population. She made it sound like a huge problem that would break Medicare and overwhelm the shrinking working class. At first it scared me - or maybe I just didn't want to be on the wrong end - then I considered what America would look like if kids weren't in charge and I became comfortable with the whole idea. The entertainment market is cornered by studios cranking out horribly trite music and movies. While there's something to be said for progress, I look forward to a day when you won't be able to make money by sticking a bikini on a 12 year old and having her shout limericks at a camera. I've been told I shouldn't complain about the quality of art that is created for children, but I'm not irritated that it doesn't entertain me - I'm irritated that it exists. The reason so many stupid people are so famous is that they have only to relate to and win over a narrow age group. I guess the eight to fourteen year old population is running this country in more ways than you'd think. Imagine if the little bastards could vote.

Even the quality of entertainment that isn't created for children is disappointing. Adults today would rather read a fantasy novel which provides an escape from this world than literature that offers a look at the universal truths of the world and of humans. The great authors today are millionaires who had a new take on magic and monsters. Gone are the days of poor, hungry, alcoholic writers who told of the real world before committing suicide by accident or on purpose. I think the art one makes is terribly limited when money is the motivation and rich people rarely have anything to say that's worth reading. Contemporary music is just as boring. Rich, famous, divorced, unapproachable people singing about "being poor" and "finding love." Philosophy died a long time ago, not because there's nothing new to say, but because no one is curious anymore about why we are the way we are. Art died even longer ago. There is no new research or new concepts. Even journalism is fantasy created for ratings. I have a friend in Vegas who once suggested to me that most TV personalities don't really believe what they're spouting - they just know it will appeal to a certain group and the advertisers will keep writing checks. I think my friend is right.

Now, I would like to backtrack to this idea of being entertained at the failings of others. It's been said before and perhaps more eloquently, but I must make this point for fear the reader will fail to understand what drives me and those who have helped shape who I am. I'm not a victim, and I don't want to come across as if I'm excusing my personal shortcomings, but I do believe that I am the product of a generation who is embarrassed by earnestness. To the frustration of our teachers and parents, our strongest held belief is that you should never be caught trying too hard. If I've already lost you, look at how we dress. Clearly a careful effort is made to look like no effort has been made. The distinction between us and the generation before us is that they really didn't seem to try or care at all. We Millennials are very clever and when we're not putting our effort into creating art, we seem to be putting it into projecting the image that our art, or knowledge, or accomplishment is more the product of effortless tinkering than of directed focus. I use myself as an example because I'm as guilty as any, but I learned from a thousand others and, no doubt, several have been influenced by me. People have told me (on occasion) that I'm "good at everything," but they don't know that it's because I only attempt things at which I know I will succeed. You'd be hard pressed to find me joining a pick-up game of basketball. The worrisome flip-side is that I/we won't attempt anything at which I'm/we're afraid there's a chance of failure. That's not entirely true, because I've been guilty of practicing in private those things which I might be asked to do in public to assure that I would succeed if put on the spot. It's quite crippling. Interestingly, what's often mistaken for humility is simply a refusal to try anything for which one has not fully prepared. A shy, "I don't know how...have him do it," when asked to draw a picture or write a poem is not a humble bow, but a nervous redirection of attention. For, what if my picture or poem doesn't impress? Even as I write this, I wonder if the reader will compare me to Tolstoy and find my work not up to par. The least disappointing formula is to stand so close to the target that you can't miss.

To my relief, and more surprisingly to my disappointment, Michael turned off the game show and put in a Hollywood feature about World War II and the conversation conceded to the sounds of explosions. I wondered if war movies were the only types that had to be dulled. Even stories based on reality usually had elements added to the big screen for entertainment value, but war movies probably are purposefully made less realistic so the focus would stay on the characters and not on the death and fear that is happening.

Adam brought us another beer and I could hear Rob starting to snore.

After the movie was over, I didn't know what time it was, but Greg went outside to smoke with Michael and I had a chance to talk to Adam. I let him tell me about college and how he came to live with these guys and how he wanted to move to California after he graduated.

When the conversation turned to Greg and I, Adam looked like he wanted to tag along. I told him he was welcome, maybe more because he had a car than for any other reason, but he was the responsible type and opted to make it to class tomorrow afternoon. Still, he would take us to Cheyenne in the morning. I thanked him for letting us stay at the house and wondered what we would be doing if Greg hadn't made friends at the coffee shop. I think it was better for Adam to offer us his couch than it was for us to accept. I'm sure we would have managed, but he needed to have a part in the adventure. It was good for his soul.

Greg and Michael came back in and Michael brought out some blankets. The recliner looked sleepable so I took my place there and let Greg have the couch. When the lights went out, I was surprised by how quiet it was. I entertained myself wondering if these guys had always existed or if they came into being just tonight and just to help us out. Not like angels - more like Schrodinger's cat. I thought Schrodinger must have been a pretty self-absorbed guy to think that the existence of something could depend so solely on him. And not like the existence of a child depends on its parents. I might have had my philosophers mixed up. Maybe the thinker's only power was in whether that cat was alive or dead - not whether it would be in the box once opened. I'm sure there was a thought along that line, too, though. It was all a very bizarre concept. The teacher of a class on philosophy in high school tried to convince me once that if you couldn't prove something didn't exist, you couldn't deny its existence. Funny how the same types dismiss the existence of God by exactly the opposite line of thinking. "The burden of proof lies on religion," they would say. I wasn't very cooperative back then, especially when a philosophy was only written so that people would have something to argue about. That's how it seemed anyway.

I got bored with the idea and tried to get comfortable on the chair.

ten

We got up the next morning and Adam let us use the shower. It's amazing how dirty you get sitting in a car for several hours a day. After we were cleaned up, Adam offered us cereal and coffee. I had awakened hungry and realized I hadn't eaten much since leaving Oregon.

The conversation at the table drifted from girls (which none of us had much to say about) to how far a guy had to drive from Laramie to find a decent place to snowboard. I didn't know whether Greg actually participated in any "extreme sports," but he always liked to talk about them. The Pacific Northwest is really the ideal place for outdoorsy folks because, depending on which direction you point the car, you're never more than an hour from surfing, skiing, or anything in between. The thought of it kind of made me regret that I always took my surroundings for granted and didn't get out more. I should really be more like the people who drive Subarus with bumper stickers supporting local beer or the up-and-coming Democratic candidate. I tried snowboarding once, but ended up breaking my friend's equipment. I think he sabotaged it so I would have to buy him a new set-up, but I never did.

Again, it looked like Adam was longing to get out of Wyoming and go see some of the country with us and again we offered. He was less sure of himself this time, but still held that he had to stay. We made an empty promise to see him again like you always make in situations like this. It's a strange social rule, but it would be stranger to admit that we would never see the kid with whom we shared coffee and beer for a day.

After feeding us, Adam got himself ready to go and Greg and I got a chance to talk about what we'd do next. Apparently the night before, Michael had told Greg all about what there was to do in Cheyenne. I tried to be excited about our adventure rather than worried about how we'd carry on without a vehicle. Greg

47

didn't seem to mind our situation and I resolved I wouldn't either.

Michael had already left for class or whatever it was he had to do. Rob came down just as we were about to leave and we thanked him for his hospitality.

"Anytime, fellas."

We repeated the promise that we'd visit although Rob seemed like a simple man and I'm sure he never lost sleep wondering if we'd follow through. Again, they probably had visitors all the time and we were just another couple dudes passing through.

We piled into Adam's car and pulled out of the long driveway. There was more traffic than I expected to see in the middle of Wyoming in February. I tried to guess where everyone was going based on their clothes and cargo, but the game got boring when it was obvious most of them were heading to their jobs in Cheyenne. I told myself I'd try again sometime when we weren't near a city.

I sat in the back so I wouldn't be expected to keep up with the discussion. Adam was telling Greg a story about one of his professors who would fall asleep mid lecture. The class would turn off the lights and leave and the professor never brought it up. Who knows if it was because he was embarrassed or just didn't care. I thought if I was a college professor, I'd just write the homework on the board every day and go home. In our age of information, it feels redundant to pay a guy to regurgitate all of the same facts and ideas that can be found online or in a book. I might even argue that you can learn the same things faster and more efficiently if you skipped out on college and spent as much time at the library.

I took notice of the moment we passed that coffee shop in Laramie. Finally, we were breaking ground again.

We made the capitol in about an hour and Adam had time before he had to get back to Laramie for class. I don't think people really worry about traffic in Wyoming. If it takes an hour to get somewhere, it takes an hour at any time of the day or night. Adam took us to another coffee shop because that's just what you do. None of us were hungry enough to go to a restaurant and it was too early to look for a bar. Greg offered that it's never too early for beer and I agreed, but Adam would be leaving town shortly so we didn't pressure him.

This cafe was a little more put together than the last one we had been to. I guess there was more competition in Cheyenne so quality was important. I've been through towns with one hospital and you can't find a single person who will say anything good about the level of care. Competition breeds quality. Maybe Greg was right to think that nothing would get done in a world where there's nothing to fight about or no one willing to throw the first punch.

"So, what are you guys going to do?" Adam may have been a bit concerned that we didn't have a car or a plan.

"Who cares?" I was trying to convince myself as much as I was trying to convince him.

"I thought maybe we'd see what kind of trouble we can find here and then head south if nothing turns up in a couple days," Greg had apparently considered our next move a little more than I thought he had.

"Well, I have the weekend off from school, so if you guys are still here on Saturday, I can come spend a couple days in Cheyenne with you."

I was glad we had something to fall back on and thanked him before getting up to add more sugar to my coffee. It still tasted like coffee and I was trying to remedy the problem.

Greg was thumbing through some biography on Winston Churchill when I came back over.

"Let's figure out something to do with all this junk," I interrupted him, smirking. "I'm not dragging these bags along behind me if we'll be walking to the East Coast." I was starting to realize, as one always does on a trip, that we'd brought too many clothes and toys. It's ironic that when packing to travel, one inevitably brings items along to keep themselves entertained. Surely, there's more to it and I shouldn't generalize, but, under examination, it seems as if we're expecting the trip to be boring and are packing accordingly. People go on cruises and bring personal sized televisions. As if the point isn't to see the world, but to watch their favorite show on a boat. I've been guilty of bringing more hours worth of reading material than the entire trip will cover. It's not because I plan on reading instead of enjoying the sights, but because I assume that hours on planes and in lobbies must be passed by being entertained rather than by meeting locals or people-watching.

Adam was amused by the idea of Greg and I hauling two bags each of things we had no intention of using over the streets of Cheyenne, and Denver, and Knoxville, Guam, Puerto Rico, Bern, Seoul, Neptune...

It was a good note to say goodbye on and Adam got up to leave as Greg and I were digging through our bags and chuckling at what we'd brought.

"I must have planned on shaving six or seven times a day."

"I don't know why you brought so many books...you can't even read," I picked on him.

"You guys should trade all that in for a skateboard or something." I kind of liked how he was thinking.

We said our goodbyes and he gave us a phone number to get him at if we were ever in the area again. Greg probably still has the phone number folded up in his wallet and may have even called Adam once or twice over the years. It seems like something he would do if he ever got drunk and had the crazy idea to catch up with old friends.

After he was gone, we decided that we'd leave our books on the shelf at the coffee shop. They could have used some new material. The clothes that we weren't wearing would be left on a bench in the park for some bum to find. Of course, this was all a temporary purging until we found ourselves something to drive or a rich widower who would take us in and will us her mansion. The latter never happened. As for the camping stove, I had never pawned anything before but was sure we could get enough out of it to buy a couple beers. At least we would use those.

I asked the well-dressed high-school kid behind the counter if he knew where the closest pawn shop was. The look on his face told me I'd just confirmed his suspicion that we were a couple of homeless crazies who had probably stolen everything we carried. We were clean, of course, but after overhearing as much as he probably had, he was entitled to think so. I didn't fault him because I'd been that put together young man a couple years before. He would probably be in my shoes in a few more. Of course, being from a "big city" of 50,000 I'm sure he'd been told his whole life that only poor people sell their stuff at pawn shops and only to buy more drugs.

"The only one in town is 8 blocks that way on the corner." He probably thought he was doing the right thing by sending us in the wrong direction. "Folks like that are what's wrong with this country," his dad had probably told him for years whenever they passed a sign-holder on the corner. "They could get a job. They just don't want to because it's easier to ask for free money. Gypsies! Thieves! I seen a bum get into the front seat of a new Cadillac once after he put in his day begging. Probably has an in-ground pool."

We stepped outside and walked down the block to the first bar we saw. The friendly bartender sent us four blocks south to the closest of three pawn shops in town and we told him we'd be back.

The greasy clerk we met at the hock shop offered six dollars for the stove. I thought we'd have better luck selling it to a sporting goods store or scrapping it but I didn't want to walk around all day for a couple extra dollars so we took the singles. No doubt he resold it the same day for $40. Pawn shops have the same advantage as scrap yards. It doesn't bother them any if you take your junk and go, but they know you need the money and can offer a fraction of what it's worth. I tried to sell him our bags, too, but he wasn't interested. We thought about leaving them with our clothes on a bench, but you're liable to attract a lot of unwanted attention for setting a bag down in public and walking away. Instead we just threw them away on our way out the door. All the miscellaneous items went in the trash, as well, and we found room in our pockets for our toothbrushes. Not entirely sanitary, but, the minimum threshold of cleanliness drops considerably on the road. Things you wouldn't consider putting in your mouth at home are fair game when you haven't showered in a few days.

We were relieved to be free of our luggage and I took comfort in the fact that if we really got ourselves stuck, we could always just hop a Greyhound straight to Portland where my parents would be glad to rescue and drive us the rest of the way home.

The part of me that wasn't terrified by all of this was proud to know that we'd really found ourselves an adventure. I wondered for a second if homeless people thought of it like that, then I realized that they don't have the novelty of a safety net and it's probably less romantic when you really, truly don't know how or whether you're going to survive.

On our way back to the bar, Greg told me about his mom and the business she started. She did something with titles or surety bonds or something like that and she was very good at it. Whatever it was, she had done her own thing then sold the business and moved to Maui because she wanted to. I started to understand that Greg wasn't lazy or crazy - he just realized that there were no rules and you could do whatever you wanted. I thought it must have been liberating to know that you were the boss of your own life and that anything was possible. Not in a cliche way like how elementary school teachers tell their students that anything is possible, but really that anything you want to do can be done and there are no rules other than those you make for yourself and force yourself to follow.

We took our places at the bar and ordered a couple micros. Portland and Denver are the international ground zeros of craft beer and we were close enough to Denver to enjoy a decent selection. It reminded me of the day less than two weeks prior that we had run into each other in Dallas and decided to get in my car and drive.

There was a different bartender and part of me felt bad that the other guy probably thought we lied about coming back. There weren't many locals in the place since it was just after noon. Greg managed to trick Marty, the bartender, out of a couple free beers by winning a bet. There was a magic trick involved where Greg pushed a coin through a dollar bill without tearing the paper money. I didn't know how he did it, but I was more interested by the fact that the Marty took the bet. He must have been new. I'm sure anyone with a couple years serving drunks would know not to play games like that. Maybe he was just feeling generous and wanted to hand out some brews. I considered telling him it was my birthday to get some more free drinks, but I thought in a place like this they would check ID to confirm. I'm not normally a liar, but when you're playing games for free beers, everything is a bet, a trick, or an illusion - never a lie.

Eventually Marty had to get back to doing real work and we were left alone. I was finishing my third beer and Greg was looking at a food menu. I think bars charge high prices for their food because they don't want to spend the time cooking and hope patrons will be deterred by sticker shock. Greg wasn't discouraged by the number next to "side of fries" and they came at the same time as our fourth drink. In the back of my mind, I was wondering how our wad of cash was looking.

~

By 7:00, Greg was darting around like I'd seen him do once or twice before. I was one beer behind, but I'm also physically larger, or I was at the time, and could put more away without losing control. I turned around to check the score on the TV and by the time I looked back, Greg was across the room asking a table full of senior citizens whether there was a good place to rent surfboards around here. I was entertained for a moment, but came to their aid when they really started to fidget. It seemed like a good time to pick up the tab and make our getaway.

Out on the street again, I opened up the atlas to Cheyenne, WY and looked for a bus symbol. I would have liked for it to have been closer, but the station was within walking distance. Everything's within walking distance when you don't have a car. Greg required some encouragement and fell in love several times on the way, but we eventually made it to the hub and planted ourselves on some corner benches. There were enough people there that I didn't think we'd be bothered by anyone with a badge as long as I could keep my drunk friend from accosting any pretty girls.

It must have been my lucky day because everyone who came through the station was either ugly, attached, or male and Greg soon fell asleep rather than endure my unwelcome voice of reason.

eleven

We woke up after more hours of sleep than I'd expected to get. It was still dark, but people were starting to arrive and get in line for the their ride to work so it couldn't have been too early. Greg looked miserable and I offered him some untimely wisdom about drinking plenty of water between beers. He didn't appreciate my help.

I left him alone to nurse his headache while I searched for a schedule. A helpful Korean War veteran showed me how to read the chart and buy my ticket from the machine. I paid for two tickets to Denver without asking Greg what he wanted to do. I was sure he'd be glad to get out of Wyoming after being at her mercy for over half of the time we'd been out of Oregon. I dropped a ticket in his lap and he grunted his approval.

We had two hours to kill before our bus would depart so I went for a walk around the station. I couldn't remember how much we'd spent the night before, but I knew it was time to get frugal. Rather than buying a paper, I read a copy of yesterday's news that someone had abandoned. The misappropriation of political contributions by some local suit was the front page story. It's always amazed me to see the majority trust in the same guys over and over. One governor is a thief, so we shift all our trust to a different candidate with essentially the same background, beliefs, and rhetoric. If the common denominator is always the same, why do we expect different results from new politicians? And every time a kid shoots up a school, it's the same story from his neighbor or grandma.

"He was always such a nice boy...he wouldn't hurt anybody...I never would have seen this coming." I'm not sure how the news outlets benefit from this worn out element to every tale of tragedy. Maybe it makes the story more remarkable and, therefore, more readable. Old people love to talk about how the news is so depressing and that the papers should produce more heartwarming stories. I guess folks don't realize that the media does exactly what is profitable and that, of course, is dictated by the readership. Kids are finding more and more that the easiest way to get famous is by killing enough people all at once that the population demands coverage - names and dates and pictures of the shooter and details of the shooter and medical diagnosis of the shooter.

I wonder how many tragedies we'd avoid if we didn't put so much trust in people with poor character. Over 50% of voters thought that Nixon was just what this country needed. Probably close to 100% of Germans thought that Hitler was the savior they'd been waiting for. Not surprisingly, Mother Teresa never got one nomination or vote for any political office. Law schools teach their students which lies you can legally get away with and lawyers are the only guys in the courtroom who don't have to promise to tell the truth. They're also among the highest paid. A police officer can find ten pounds of heroin on any dirtbag, but if the paperwork isn't in line, it's inadmissible. What becomes most important isn't that someone broke the law, but whether the proper hoops were jumped through. And if they weren't, there are no consequences for the obviously guilty. Big oil doesn't pay taxes and the logic is that, if they did, the price of the product would increase to make up for higher overhead. If threatening to wreck the system gets you a better deal, maybe I can get out of paying taxes by promising not to burn down a preschool.

I've had this conversation a hundred times and the solution settled on is always that everyone should just do the right thing. And, because that's the solution, it will never happen. Morality can't be legislated. Only certain actions can be criminalized and I think the people at which the laws are aimed are the exact people who won't follow them anyway. Really, the only thing that can be affected by legislation is which consequences will be distributed for which actions. Laws only echo social norms. The innocent don't need the rules written down because they already know what's right and wrong. It's all very circular.

It felt strange not bringing anything on the bus with me. We found our seats towards the back and Greg tried to go back to sleep. For a while I was interested in the scenery outside, but it all looked the same and I eventually got bored. I wished for a second that I'd kept just one book for such an occasion, then realized that I didn't want to merely pass the time.

The gentleman across the aisle was from a generation who

passed the time on planes and trains and buses by talking to the guy in the next seat over. We shared some small talk about where we were from and where we were going. His brother worked for a non-profit in Denver and he was going to help out with some big event they were having. I told him Greg and I were meandering somewhere and we'd know it when we got there. He reminded me of my dad. I could tell he thought the idea was a little weird, but wouldn't expressly discourage it. The further across the country we got, the more surprised I was that people were so shocked at us not having a plan. It seemed like 60 or 90 years ago, it was just what you did. If something wasn't working out in Oklahoma, you sold the house, packed all the kids into your sedan, and headed west until someone gave you a job. Maybe prosperity has paralyzed us. Now, it's only the young and crazy or the wasted homeless who would consider packing up and searching for something better somewhere else. The more money a man has, the more attached he is to his home, it seems. Money's only good for a couple things, one of which is walling yourself in with fancy toys to keep the world out. And it's really just a disservice to yourself. The more comfortable one becomes in the world they've built, the less likely they are to survive if things fall apart.

The ride was around two hours long and Greg never opened his eyes the whole time. I regretted sitting near the toilet and wondered why some people can't wait a couple hours for the sake of the rest of us. Bad planning, I guessed.

The air in Denver was much colder than what we'd left in Cheyenne. It was still before noon, but Greg was apparently starting to feel better. Or maybe he was just glad to be in a new place. The bus station in Denver was much bigger than the one we'd departed from and we sat down for some sandwiches before going all the way outside.

"I wonder how much money we have." I was surprised that he cared.

"Probably a few hundred still," I was being optimistic. "I'm still expecting my last paycheck from one of my jobs." My parents were going to wire me the money when it came, but I had just realized that I hadn't talked to them since we left. Other than them probably thinking I was dead, there was the problem of them not knowing where to send the money when it arrived.

"I was thinking about having my family put my truck up for sale. I don't want to go back to Dallas anytime soon. It'll probably take a couple weeks to sell, but we'll be needing the money by then."

It was decided that we'd find a phone and check in with our families. A few years later near Mount Saint Helens, a gas station attendant would tell me that pay phones had been replaced by cell phones. We didn't realize at the time, but we were lucky to find one at the bus depot in Denver.

I called first and my dad answered. He didn't push too hard for details about the trip and I was glad to leave out that we had sold the car and slept in a bus station. My paycheck had come and it was less than I thought it should have been. I told him to hang onto it and I'd let him know in a few days when I needed it. He was glad that he was guaranteed to get another call in the near future. I tried not to care what he'd think about us hitchhiking and selling our belongings for beer money, but you always want to make Dad proud. My only hope was that Mom would answer the phone next time. She could relay our misfortune and I would be spared the interrogation.

Greg called his family and had no reservations about sharing the details of our adventure. I walked outside with the map book to figure out where we were and he joined me after a few minutes. It had been arranged that his dad would put a sign on the truck and drive it around until it sold. Unfortunately, he would have to ask for less than it was worth to hope for a quick sale.

Our attention was jerked from the atlas when a couple guys started yelling at each other across the street. The older one had parked too close to the nice car belonging to the younger and now the younger couldn't get out. A bike cop passing by stopped to calm things down because every disagreement warrants police intervention in our modern society. My dad and his brother still tell stories about their teachers in high school who would allow, even encourage students finish a fight they had gotten into over a girl or whatever. I wondered what police used to do before everything was illegal.

We wandered through shops and crowds for most of the day and maintained a running commentary on the people and stores that we passed. It was liberating to be the only guys on the street with nowhere to get to. For a moment in the early afternoon, I thought I'd lost Greg, but found him two doors back talking to a guy with dreadlocks. Every twenty-something in Denver wants dreadlocks.

Greg was asking the hippy where to see live music in

Denver on a Thursday night and the hippy was moving around more than a person should and clicking his teeth to the beat of a song that no one else could hear. It was apparently very amusing to Greg and he started slapping his knees to a matching beat. The whole thing was really a sight and a few middle-aged, middle class women averted their eyes as they rushed passed probably trying to make it home in time to see their favorite show.

"I got your live music right here, Maaaaannnnn..." the hippy managed to spit out in between bars. I wasn't sure if Greg could really relate or if he was just making a game of the whole thing. I tried to imagine what kind of worldview you'd have to have for this to seem normal, as the hippy apparently did. I remembered going to church with my parents as a kid and seeing a drunk guy get up and start preaching. The pastor quickly shooed him away and said that we should be "in the spirit - not the SPIRITS." I don't know if it was a play on words, or if the two are similar enough that he had to make the distinction.

People will do things in church on Sunday that they wouldn't do anywhere else and you can get away with things on the football field that would get you arrested any other time.

Well, Hemingway did say, "when you laugh, laugh like hell. And when you get angry, get good and angry." And he's more famous than Kipling so maybe he's right. At least more relatable, which is the same thing. Maybe I'm strange for being so even-tempered.

I didn't feel bad for not joining in the madness, but I wondered what people thought when they saw me. Did they think I was just an observer who was standing too close? I feel the same way about dancing at weddings.

By the time the hippy was rolling around on the sidewalk and mumbling and spitting and kicking, we realized that we wouldn't get a real answer to Greg's question.

As we walked away, a business owner came out and started yelling at the hippy to move along. He had probably watched the whole thing, but was less intimidated telling only one crazy to leave. His plea fell on deaf ears, and I'm sure the hippy is still there today beating his head on the pavement to the tune of some Bob Dylan song that no one really likes.

If the event had no other effect, Greg was now determined to find a show. It was starting to get dark and we didn't walk much further before we heard live music coming from a crowded doorway down the block. Live music never sounds good when heard through walls and from a distance so we took a chance and weren't disappointed when we got inside. The place was full of twenty-two year olds wearing sunglasses and tight pants. We figured this must have been a popular local band or they had a lot of friends and it was probably the former because the music was done well. I started to think that when people in Denver decided to do something, they did it all the way.

We ordered some cheap beers and stood near the wall. The lead singer was completely incoherent, but I could see some fans singing along so there must have been words. Three years later, the band would have a top 40 hit, but they didn't last long when the frontman's drug habit interfered with contractual obligations. Rock stars must walk a fine line between being "with it" enough to deal with managers and record companies but out of their minds enough to relate to their millions of stoned, screaming fans. I could never do it. Then there's the issue of losing your fan base as soon as you get popular. Almost universally, the fans who like a band when it starts out are the same ones who won't stick around because they pride themselves on liking bands that aren't well-known. I often hear that a band has "sold out," but I think that's just the excuse most often used when a fan knows it's time to disassociate from a musician who has made it big.

We weren't really dressed the part but one kid did come and talk to us. He was confused about the lineup and asked if we knew which band this was. I thought he must have been drunk or insane because a glance at us should have told him that we were the least informed, most out of place guys in the room. Or, maybe for just that reason we were the most approachable.

His name was Andrew and he was from someplace in Ohio that has no historical significance, but has a great little teriyaki joint on the edge of town. He had flown to Denver two days ago to see a girl he'd met online, but she turned out to be a liar and he was stuck in the city until his flight out next week. I guessed Denver's not a bad place to be stuck. He said it wasn't all that bad meeting the girl. She wasn't a man and she didn't kill him like everyone thinks will happen when you meet someone online. The problem was that you can be anyone you want behind the cloak of a computer and she didn't turn out to be as charming or as lovely or as single as she had pretended to be. Andrew wasn't the most beautiful person, either, but you always want to side with the underdog and he had taken quite a chance coming out here. He was a tall kid and I wondered how he kept track of his feet, them being so far away from his eyes.

We talked for a while when we could hear each other over the music. Greg wandered across the room to talk to a girl who looked 14, but left her alone once her boyfriend came back from the bathroom.

Andrew was staying at a youth hostel downtown since it hadn't worked out to stay with his lady-friend. We hadn't considered the option until then, but thought it might be nice to pay a few bucks for a bed rather than sleeping on a bench again (on returning home, certain family members mixed up hostel with brothel and I had to explain that I hadn't spent the night in a whorehouse).

We had a couple more beers and left when the place started smelling like sweat and vomit. When they get drunk, hipsters really aren't any classier than the rest of the world. The band must have been drinking, too, because the music got progressively worse. Maybe they just weren't trying as hard because they knew the drunk crowd wouldn't notice.

It had gotten a lot colder outside since we'd gone in. I was glad we wouldn't be out in it for very long and I resolved that if we didn't head for warmer weather soon, I would invest in a coat.

Rather than walking, we paid a dollar to ride the bus and it dropped us off right in front of the place where Andrew was staying. It was a short ride, but there was enough time for Greg to tell a story about seeing a drunk guy who was trying to light the wrong end of a cigarette at the bar we'd just left. It was funnier than it should have been and I got a grasp on Andrew's sense of humor. The kid was obviously glad to have some friends to talk to after wandering around Denver for the last couple days. We tried to ask him what he had found to do, but it sounded like he wasn't really the type to go looking for a good time. Apparently just going to that bar to see a band that he had heard of in passing was a big step out of his comfort zone. I wondered how a homebody like Andrew could bring himself to fly a thousand miles to meet a girl he'd never seen. I guess loneliness will do strange things to a man. Unfortunately, the undesirable outcome would probably teach him not to take big chances anymore. Part of me hoped that we could turn his trip around and that he wouldn't regret making such a crazy move.

We made it inside the hostel and must have gotten the last two beds because as we were walking up the stairs towards the dorm, I could hear the owner telling the next guy that there was nothing available. Maybe they screened their patrons and the bum asking for a bed didn't meet the requirements.

A bulletin board on the way up the stairs offered rideshares, guitar lessons, and meal coupons for local restaurants.

Greg flopped down on a bed against the wall and I took one nearby. It looked like there were a lot of empty beds, but I figured everyone was like us and didn't have any possessions. Andrew confirmed for us that no one had been in these two beds the night before.

After claiming our beds, the three of us went further upstairs to the kitchen and Andrew handed us each a beer out of the fridge. I'd never stayed in a hostel in the States before. I found it to be a lot like places I'd stayed in Europe, probably because the same types of people run and patronize hostels so they all have a similar feel.

Someone said something that got us all started on politics and it was a lively conversation since Andrew was from the opposite side of the country than us. I wondered if Andrew watched different news than us or if his proximity to D.C. gave him a different perspective. It's amazing how opposing parties find different details of the same story to be true and important. Greg was going on about weapons of mass destruction and Andrew was talking about the responsibility of a world power to stand up to tyranny. They were really agreeing on everything, but from different angles, so they didn't realize it. When discussions turn into who's right or wrong, I become useless because I'm too willing to see things from the other side. I would be a horrible politician.

A couple of Australian girls came into the kitchen just in time and Greg lost interest in the conversation.

Andrew and I chatted a little more about foreign policy before joining the three across the room. Greg was telling the Aussies about breaking down on the side of I-80 somewhere in Wyoming and walking to the nearest town. They seemed very impressed with his embellished story of adventuring across the country. I didn't remember there being quite as many near-death experiences, but his version of the story was more exciting than my memory of events so I listened as intently as our foreign friends. I wondered if they thought it was strange that I was so captivated by a story in which I was a main character.

When it was their turn to tell how they'd ended up here, the older of the two talked about coming to snowboard and stay with an American cousin. Until then, I'd wondered why anyone would leave Australia and visit Colorado in the middle of Winter. They were staying in town tonight and their family would come meet them in the morning to go to the mountains.

We all talked and laughed for a couple hours and I could tell that Greg was torn about which one he loved more. He wasn't particularly fond of blondes - which they both were - but the fact that they were from the other side of the world and had sexy accents trumped their hair color.

When Andrew ran out of beer, we all moved to a pub next door to the hostel. There was no live music at this place, and therefore no one was wearing sunglasses, but the PA was playing plenty of bad music and we all had a good laugh every time a Nickelback song came on. It might have been a big, ironic game, but the bar didn't seem to cater to that type of crowd, so we assumed the bartender really wanted to listen to the station that was playing. The girls taught us a game that involved toothpicks and napkins and Andrew beat us all. I think they were going easy on us, but my hands wouldn't do what I told them to and I kept dropping the toothpicks on the floor.

"You know the hardest part about getting a drunk guy drunk?" Andrew asked anyone who was listening.

The quieter of the two girls wasn't very quiet anymore and threw a toothpick at him which I think meant she wanted him to finish the joke.

"First you have to get him sober!"

Greg drank to that and promised that he'd buy Andrew a Russian mail-order bride so he wouldn't have to meet girls online anymore.

I'm having a hard time remembering the rest of the night, but I do remember losing Greg after another hour. I also recall Andrew breaking something and one of the girls falling off a chair. Eventually the bartender either kicked us out or we got tired and walked back to our hostel and up the stairs. I sat down on the wrong bed at first and a Swedish guy yelled at me in German. I don't know any German swear words, but I could tell he was saying something rude about my mother. I saw the guy the next morning, but thought that apologizing would be confessing to the crime.

twelve

Greg must have made it back at some point during the night because he was there snoring when I woke up. I decided that if I ever ran a hostel, it would have a guard in the dorm who would shoot anyone who snored or talked too loudly before noon. I've always found that I'm generally happier if I wake up early and start my day, but that doesn't make it any easier.

I soon gave up trying to drown out the chatting and banging around above us in the kitchen and got up and showered. I found some free coffee down in the lobby and drank it on purpose. While I was choking the tarry liquid down, I looked at the bulletin board again and considered calling for guitar lessons. I've heard girls love guys who play guitar. Or maybe that's just something ugly people say to explain why they don't have a girlfriend. If they would just learn to strum, they'd never be lonely again. Maybe I would skip the lessons and just lie that I could play. As long as no one produced an instrument, I would never have to deliver.

One of the rideshare ads caught my eye and I waded through the poor grammar. Someone was driving to Indiana on Monday (I didn't know if it was this Monday or last Monday or some Monday in 2015). I wondered what people do in Indiana in the Winter when it's too cold to grow corn. Probably make cornbread. Or whiskey. The ad didn't look like it had been there long and I tore it away from its staples to show Greg. He was still out cold, but Andrew's bed was empty and I found him in the kitchen wondering where the food and beer with his name on it had gone. The girls were there and they made pancakes for us. I'm embarrassed to say I was a little bit pleased that Greg was elsewhere and the four of us could enjoy breakfast. Andrew and I were much more popular with the girls when Greg wasn't out-charming us.

We talked about kangaroos and surfing and Andrew embarrassed himself once by asking what language they speak in Australia. I wondered what Greg would talk with them about if he was up, but the conversation was pleasant enough, although never riveting.

After a while, the girls had to go meet their cousin, but said they'd see us around. I thought they were just saying that because it's what people say, but later I would learn that Greg had exchanged contact information the night before and promised that we'd all come visit them in Sydney that Summer. We never did.

Greg got up just after they left. It was almost poetic. We gave him the last of the pancakes and lied that we hadn't seen the girls all morning. We weren't being nice - we just didn't want to hear about how we should have woken him up. Again, Greg had a headache and I was starting to see a pattern. I showed him the paper with the ride offered to Indiana and he asked what we would do there.

"I'm just really hungry for corn, Man."

Andrew appreciated my response more than Greg did, but Greg agreed that it was as good of an idea as any. Probably more because he didn't want to do any critical thinking in his present state than because he actually thought Indiana would be interesting. I wasn't even sure it was a current ad, but I told him I'd send a message to the email address and see what happened.

While Greg drank coffee in the kitchen and found his way out of his fog from the night before, I went down to the lobby again this time to use the shared computer. I sent the email and took advantage of the opportunity to call my mom and have her send the money from my paycheck since it seemed like we'd be in Denver for a couple of days. I was sure we were running out of cash and told myself we wouldn't buy any four-dollar beers that night.

I got off the computer when I saw a tourist type sitting too close and glancing at me every few seconds. He wasn't very subtle and I wondered what he could possibly need to do so urgently that required a computer connected to the internet. Probably had to update his followers on where he was that day and which museums/architectural wonders/attractions he had seen. I was reminded that some people only travel, not so much to see, but so they can tell others what they've seen.

When I got back upstairs, Greg was in the bathroom puking and Andrew was putting up with an artist who never got around to sketching anything and was sharing all the reasons why he couldn't. It's funny how many artists you run into who are waiting for things to fall into place just right before they create anything.

"I'm just saving up money for my new apartment...then I'll have space to paint," or "after I get a new job and buy a car, then I'll be able to go out and take pictures." It makes it easy to be ahead in the art world - and life, I guess - when one has only to make any effort in some direction. I've heard it said that it's so hard to stand out these days because so many people are doing so many things and there's nothing new under the sun. The people who say this are the ones who wouldn't even be successful if they were the only poet in the world because they would find an excuse not to write.

It made me think of my sister's husband who I've mentioned is a musician. He may be the most honest artist I've ever met for this reason: he makes a habit of not listening to very much music. It's not because he is concerned that he will be judged for his taste like is true of most musicians who are motivated by reputation, but so that he won't be influenced to write with a certain style. The logic is that it's easier not to sound like anyone else when you don't know what anyone else sounds like. Yeah...he's either very honest and committed to his art, or he's insane. For the record, I lean towards admiring him as earnest and humble, but he still may very well be completely mad. One would have to be to marry my sister. And my respect for him doesn't stop me from repeating the joke for acquaintances unfamiliar with my family that my brother-in-law is a musician who doesn't listen to music. Although the joke has lost some of its punch since it has come into vogue to claim to paint but not be able to name a single well-known painter or to write, never having read anything that can be counted as literature.

I skipped joining the artist's audience and laid down on my bed to rest my eyes. The events of the last week played out in my head and I wondered how things would have been different if one detail was changed. Where would we be if the coin flip had sent us south? Or if I was awake and keeping up on Dave's oil consumption in his last hours? It seemed like we'd been gone a month already, but it wasn't even the weekend yet. Maybe we should have taken Greg's truck. It probably would have lasted longer than the 24 hours that Dave made it. I wondered what my family and co-workers were doing back in Dallas. Probably nothing. Probably watching TV. I wondered what my Grandpa was doing. There was no one in the world who I looked up to more than my Grandpa. I was never really the sentimental type, but I hoped he knew and I hoped I'd figure out how to tell him someday. I wasn't exactly homesick, but you naturally wonder how things are getting along without you.

Greg came out of the bathroom looking sweatier, but in better spirits. I told him that I'd sent the email and that we had some money coming from home. Just then, a staff member came in to get the dorm back in shape after it was destroyed by 20 drunk travelers. She told us we had to be gone during the middle of the day and could come back in at 5:00. Andrew took the opportunity to attach to us on our way outside and abandon the lazy artist.

None of us were hungry and the sun was out so we found a park to bum around in. I was content to people watch, and Greg joined some other guys throwing around a Frisbee. Andrew was thinking or daydreaming about something, but I didn't bother to ask what.

I've heard that if you don't like the weather in Denver, just wait 15 minutes and it will change. Well, it was a cloudless day and we were glad that the only way the weather changed was by getting warmer.

We spent most of the day like that and picked up the money my mom had sent on the way back to the hostel. Greg paid for three more nights while I got back on the computer to look for an email. I expected a message that would say the guy left weeks ago and forgot to take his ad down, but there was nothing new.

Andrew was due to fly out on Wednesday so we spent our days with him while we all waited for our exit from Colorado. Not that we were trying to escape. Friday night we went to bed early and on Saturday morning we had breakfast with a 40-something couple who was backpacking across the U.S. I'd heard of backpacking Europe, but never America. They were from Vermont and were right on schedule for their mid-life crisis. She made an excellent omelet, and I went out and bought some pastries to contribute. They told us that the goal of life shouldn't just be to live as long as possible, but it seems that's what it has become. Researchers and governments and healthcare providers spend so much time and money and thought on prolonging life, but if your life isn't worth living in the first place, how do you benefit from increasing its length? I had never considered the idea and was intrigued. I thought of brain-dead 100 year olds living in nursing homes where the only real goal was to keep them from dying. It's no wonder so many people live so madly. They don't want their bodies to out-survive their brains. I realized that I'd never been physically injured and that it probably said a lot about how I use my body. It worried me to think that I would be one of the old folks with no medical problems and a demented brain.

The more we talked to them, the more I realized that they weren't the typical mid-life "crisis-ers." They were making a concerted effort to live boldly but maintained a healthy balance of being content with how things were turning out. I thought maybe the husband, Todd, was the guy who Peter Meinke wrote about:

"Therefore, marry a pretty girl
After seeing her mother;
Show your soul to one man,
Work with another;
And always serve bread with your wine.
But son, always serve wine."

We got lost on the East side of town that afternoon and made a game out of not stopping to ask for directions. I think someone once said that if you don't know where you're going, any road will take you there. That sort of summed up our situation. We stopped at a pizza place for dinner and were suddenly glad to have gotten lost. It was dark and we were too full to think very hard. Andrew asked a cop how to get back to where we came from and he pointed in the opposite direction than we thought we had to go. We finally got back home and stayed up late in the kitchen talking to an Asian kid who didn't have an Asian accent. It seemed like the kitchen was the best place to meet people.

The email never came and we went back to the bulletin board on Sunday. Most of the ads were written by hitchhikers asking for a free ride to anywhere, but an ad that hadn't been there before offered a ride to North Carolina leaving the next afternoon. It had better contact information and I was able to track down the guy by asking the lady behind the desk downstairs. Apparently, he had been sleeping three beds away from me all along, and Greg and Andrew and I sat in the bar next door and talked to him for several hours that night. His name was Kyle and he looked exactly like a Kyle. He was short with big trendy hair and a very deliberate 7 o'clock shadow. Looking at him reinforced my belief that people turn into the name that their parents give them. He had a lot of stories for how young he was and I believed about half of the details. More than anything, I was entertained to see him and Greg try to out story each other. He had some kind of involvement in the Air Force Academy or he was trying to get in - I wasn't really sure by his vague mention of it. I gathered that he was driving home to North Carolina to ask his parents for money. He was obviously an only child.

My old friend, Jordan, pointed out to me once that most people just want to be entertained. He had a habit of asking kids what they would do if they won the lottery and, overwhelmingly, the answer was that they'd buy houses and cars and basketball teams. Without realizing it, their answers essentially meant spending the rest of their lives without doing anything noble or productive. The more I got to know Kyle over the next couple of days, the more I realized Jordan was right and Kyle was one of those people. Maybe I was, too, because I would probably choose to have fun and be comfortable if I won a million dollars.

On an only semi-related note, it's funny to me how much praise rich people get for donating to charities. I agree that it's a good thing, but when it's such a small part of your fortune, it's not really a sacrifice. If Bono gave a millions dollars and I gave one dollar to the same cause, he would probably be considered more of a philanthropist even though it was the same percentage of our "fortunes." I think I learned about a similar story in Sunday school once.

Anyway, Kyle taught me a lot about myself over the next couple of days, most of which I can't articulate, but it's there.

Andrew couldn't be convinced to come with us, so we said our goodbyes on Monday and packed ourselves into Kyle's coupe. Greg kept with his tradition of exchanging contact information and promising to visit.

The car was less rickety than Dave, but not by much. It shook violently whenever the brakes were applied and most of the warning lights on the dash were on. I fully expected to get stranded again. We planned on making the trip in three days and Kyle seemed happy to drive the whole way. I picked up a tech magazine at our gas stop on the way out of town but never read much past the table of contents. The cover is always so much more interesting than the articles. Greg and Kyle were debating which superhero was best and I stayed out of it because I couldn't see any sense in preferring one made up character over another.

We took I-70 East out of Colorado and across Kansas. Coming down from the high altitude of Denver had a surprising impact on the climate and everything became a little more dreary. Kyle said that it was because we were farther away from the sun and I think he really believed that. It rained all the way through Kansas and for most of the next three days. Halfway through Kansas, we filled up and took 35 South towards Oklahoma City. Kyle was making good time and hadn't stopped talking for hours. I noticed that when he got excited about something, he seemed to drive faster. I came up with a plan to keep him worked up and see if we could make the coast in two days, but it sounded like too much trouble. Greg was talking a lot, too. Everything they discussed was a competition. Sometimes I could tell one of them was taking a side he didn't believe in just for the sake of argument. Maybe they both understood that a conversation is lifeless if everyone agrees on the points.

It was dark when we came through Oklahoma City, but Kyle didn't look like he had any intention of stopping. He reminded me of every short person I'd ever met. The big city whizzed by and Kyle put the car into an all-wheel slide the entire length of the ramp for I-40. I wondered how his brakes ever got so bad when he clearly didn't use them. In between hollering about the virtue of music from the 50s, he explained to me that gas was always cheaper outside of the city and we'd wait another hundred miles before filling up again. Greg took the position that real music never existed until the 60s and that fuel could be had for a dollar per gallon cheaper in the heart of a metropolis. I didn't know about the whole music thing because I liked modern music (which I didn't admit), but I was pretty sure Greg was right about gas being cheaper where there's more competition.

Kyle came to a stop in Fort Smith just over the Arkansas border and I think it was the first time in five hours that we got under 90 miles per hour. It was Kyle's turn to pay for gas and Greg followed him into the service station to continue their debate about whether the royal family of England really wielded any political power anymore. I took a walk around the parking lot to get my land legs back before going in to find some food.

The fat man behind the counter gave us each wrong change and I wondered if he was really a genius and was going to retire early with all the extra quarters he tricked people out of. On the way back to the car, I did some basic math to figure out how many people would have to come through for him to steal a million dollars worth of quarters. My dad always says that you can't retire on a million, but I'd give it a good shot if I ever had the opportunity.

Kyle bought an energy drink and tried to convince us that caffeine had the opposite effect on him and would put him to sleep.

For the first time that day, the three of us started to wonder how we would sleep in the small car. We found a park in town and Kyle pulled the car under a tree. I wasn't sure what the logic was. We all got out and smoked cigars in the bathroom which was the only dry place in the park. Greg had quit smoking cigarettes as quickly as he had started. Kyle asked me if I had a girlfriend and I was surprised he cared what anyone else had to say. That seems harsh, and I don't mean it rudely, but I hadn't been expecting any questions from him and wasn't prepared to answer. Maybe his jaw was getting tired.

"No, Dude. Love is a digestive disorder...you can't eat or sleep, but it goes away eventually."

You'll be happy to know that years later, I don't think that anymore and am very pleased with how things have turned out.

I realized love was the only thing I hadn't heard Kyle and Greg debate. Maybe because they shared the same opinion and it wouldn't have made a very good argument.

We all stood for a minute smoking our cigars in silence.

They both started talking at the same time and Greg let Kyle go ahead.

"Yeah, I don't have one either, but there's this girl back at home and we've been on and off..." and so on and so on. It was the story I had expected. He wasn't exactly the picture of stability, but he was an attractive guy and I knew he wouldn't have any problems settling down if he ever decided he was ready.

Greg's story was the opposite in some ways. He'd had many girlfriends but maybe was expecting something more ideal than is possible. I knew he would do well someday, too, and it made me glad to know that I was on this adventure with two guys who would be successful in life. It was more than I could say for most of my friends back home. For what it's worth, that was the moment I realized that Greg and I had become friends.

fourteen

I won't say we woke up the next morning because that would suggest we slept. When it got light, we gave up on trying to sleep and got back on the road. It was hard enough for Greg and I to sleep in the Ford, but with three of us in a coupe, it was impossible. Kyle stayed in the driver's seat which was probably the hardest place to sleep. I was next to him in the front which wasn't much easier other than I didn't have a steering wheel to contend with. Even Greg - in the back seat - couldn't find a position that was conducive to sleeping and the rain outside made sure that even if we got comfortable enough, it would still be too loud to doze off. I imagine it would have been a sight for anyone passing by seeing three grown men trying to sleep in a car that was only as spacious as our combined volume. Probably a lot like how I imagine a clown car would look without the face paint.

Kyle was the first to give up on sleeping so naturally he thought it was time to start talking. That signaled the end of Greg's and my attempts. I was in a bad mood, so I tried to keep my mouth shut. I had resolved at an early age that I wouldn't take out my bad attitude on other people. I think one of the meanest things you can do is to be an asshole to people who have nothing to do with your breakdown and then refuse to talk about it so they end up thinking they're the problem.

We payed perfectly good money for something that passed for coffee on our way out of town (although I'm not a very good judge). Kyle ordered something that I couldn't have pronounced at the time and have now forgotten entirely. I thought he probably liked saying the name more than he actually enjoyed the drink. In recent years, I've researched the coffee culture a little because I just don't get it and have been amused to find that a lot of the terms are completely unrelated to, if not the opposite of, their original meaning. For example, a macchiato in the original language meant a shot of espresso that was "marked" with a dollop of foam, but in the American vernacular, it has come to mean almost nothing more than a fancy word to use when ordering. A caramel macchiato here and now is merely a caramel and vanilla latte - very far from a shot of espresso with perhaps half an ounce of cream or foam. In fact, if you order a caramel vanilla latte, you'll get exactly the same drink made the same way as if you'd ordered a caramel macchiato. The only difference is that you'll feel less sophisticated ordering your drink. Ironically, the word sophisticated has even been used incorrectly in recent history and originally meant to falsify or turn things around for the sake of tricking. Sophisticated folks were manipulators, but the modern definition has more to do with being classy. Again, the people who perpetuate this are the same people who can't see the irony.

We got back on the road and it was Tuesday. It felt more like the end of the week, but then, the beauty of having nowhere to be is that you lose your sense of time and place.

I-40 jogged South just North of Little Rock and Kyle took us through the capitol. I was surprised by how many people were out walking in the rain. The people in Little Rock looked taller than everywhere else we'd been, but I attributed it to our car riding lower to the ground or maybe they really were. Kyle was telling me about how our forefathers would have been hung for treason if we'd lost the war. I already knew the story, but let him tell it anyway because he seemed to think he was divulging a little-known secret. The situation was akin to letting someone finish a joke to which you already know the punchline. I think he must have been excited about the whole thing because he was driving well over the speed limit and missed the exit for I-40 out of town and had to backtrack. I used to work with a lady named Jill who couldn't do two things at once. I think that Kyle had the same problem, or his priorities were just different. Greg was still trying to sleep in the back seat, but was being tossed around by Kyle's wild lane changes. It was a wonder that Kyle knew where he was going with the signs flying by so fast.

I thought I saw one of my uncles in the car next to us as we passed it on the right, but when I looked back, it was just an old Asian woman.

We made Tennessee before noon about the time Greg was starting to wake up and talk about food.

The 40 would have taken us straight to Nashville which is

the Portland of the South (or maybe Portland is the Nashville of the North) but coming through Memphis, Kyle swerved and just made the 78 ramp towards Alabama and Georgia. He said he wanted to see if it's true what they say about Atlanta traffic.

~

Kyle finally agreed to stop for gas and lunch after another hour. The town was called New Albany and I wondered where Old Albany was. Maryland? Probably not. Kyle dropped us off to save a seat at some burger joint while he drove down the road and fueled up. The menu looked the same as every menu at every burger restaurant across the country. The waitress was cute and must have been new enough that she wasn't worn out or jaded yet. Greg managed to charm her out of a free side of fries.

After lunch, we walked to the grocery store next door and Greg bought beer and cigarettes. I asked him if he was going to start smoking again and he said that he wasn't but that cigarettes are currency on the road. I think he was mistaking the road for prison. In the real world, people ask you for a cigarette and you give it to them for free. It's not like prison where you can trade for something else because the bums who ask you for a cigarette have nothing to give in return.

None of us really wanted to get back into the car, so we hung around in the parking lot for a while and laughed at a dog across the street who was trying to climb over a fence that he could have walked around. Kyle told a story about how his mom used to collect pets and at one time they had two dogs, three cats, two birds, a hamster, a frog, a rabbit, and a tank of fish. Neither Greg nor I could beat that so we conceded that he held the record. Greg told a story about a guy who had an apartment full of exotic pets that apparently staged a coup one day and ate him. The cops responded out when his family hadn't heard from him in a week and broke down his door to find dozens of snakes and spiders picking the last of the dude's meat off his bones.

In another three hours we were in Birmingham and the rain had let up. Greg was still in the back seat and had been drinking beer since our last stop. Whenever we passed a semi, he tried to climb up into the front seat to give them the signal to honk their big horn. I was tired of getting stepped on, so I'd taken to punching him in the arms whenever they got close enough. Once, he didn't think about where he was grabbing and his hand landed on the steering wheel and he almost pulled us into the driver's door of a late-model BMW. I almost offered to switch seats with him, but I didn't think Kyle would want him up front.

In Birmingham, Kyle took us straight to a fancy hotel so his car would be valet parked. We walked into the hotel to keep up the act and went straight out the back entrance on the other side of the lobby. I doubt we were fooling anyone with our unkempt hair and the stale smell of beer and restaurant food. Although maybe that's exactly the type who patronizes hotels. Now that I think about it, everyone probably just thought we were careening towards the end of a week long bachelor party.

Back outside, Kyle and I were enjoying a street performer's show while Greg wandered into an alley and asked a homeless woman if he could borrow her cell phone. He must not have had any luck, because he wandered out more quickly than he'd gone in. There was a crowd of people gathered down the street and in Greg's current mood, everything was interesting and exciting so he headed that way and we tagged along.

We didn't have to get very close to know what was going on. A gentleman with the biggest beard I'd ever seen and with clothes that were all the same color of brown - due to use more than design - was enlightening passersby about the similarities between America and Sodom and Gomorrah. I wondered if he was homeless because he believed in what he was preaching, or if he'd come to believe in it after first becoming homeless. Well, Jesus did say to sell everything and "follow me."

I expected Birmingham to be a lot more down home and apple pie, but it was turning out to be more like how I'd pictured New York City to be. I'd never been to New York City, but had seen enough movies to believe that everyone there was either homeless, loud, or both.

We quickly got bored and made our way down the street, not really aiming for any place in particular. We stopped at a bagel shop and watched the ambulances scream past. I wondered what the big hurry was and assumed that someone somewhere was dying.

Greg was sobering up and talking to the bagel girl. She was very impressed that we had come so far across the country and he was making a game out of talking her into coming with us as he'd done everywhere else we'd stopped. Again, she had some kind of obligations at home that none of us believed were really that important. I don't think I've ever heard a good reason for why someone couldn't see the world. Money, I guess. The best reason anyone has given that they can't quit their job and see the country is money. But, even then, you tend to find a way if you're motivated. I once talked to a guy in Toledo, Spain who drew pictures for tourists and no one ever realized that he himself was a tourist with a clever way of making money to get to the next town. It's easy to tell when someone really doesn't want to travel because they get annoyed when you try to help them figure out a way to pay for it.

Incidentally, I've realized as I'm writing this that during our trip I never had any intention of putting the events of our adventure into a book. And I think that's the best way. I probably would have had entirely different goals along the way and would have missed out on opportunities while trying to force an interesting story. I don't know how to say it, but my point is that you may create a better story if you don't think of it in terms of a story while it's happening. You'd be too distracted by the elements to appreciate them. It seems that so often the people who want to write a story don't have anything to say and the people with the best stories never write them down because they're too busy living. This is a good problem. I guess the hope is that those who do live will be moved later to tell the story that they were a part of and I hope mine is worth reading now that I'm putting it to paper after these years.

We were bored of watching traffic after a while and Greg had realized that Cutie wasn't very bright. You can only talk to a dumb person for so long even when they're attractive. I think he and I had the same thought that it was a good thing she wasn't coming with us because he didn't play the game as frequently from then on.

I'm not so much of an introvert that I need alone time every day, but I realized that it had been over a week since I'd gotten away from everyone. We made plans to meet back at the fancy hotel in two hours and I walked in the opposite direction from them.

Nothing noteworthy happened as I walked around downtown and I wondered if Greg's presence was the only reason anything interesting had gone on since we left Oregon. I was glad to have him along and wondered where I'd be without him. Probably sleeping in my broken down car in Wyoming for about the eighth night in a row. Really, I was okay with not running into any trouble for a couple hours. I did buy a paper and a bottled water and found a bench where I could catch up on the news of the world. It was exactly as I'd expected. Maybe my dad was right that the world's unsafe and that everyone's out to get you. Or maybe he read too many newspapers. The chicken or the egg.

When the news got boring, I tried to compile a list of phrases that seemed redundant.

1. Mailman (Male-man)
2. Corn maze (Corn-maize)

I couldn't think of more than two, but liked the idea and resolved to keep it in the back of my mind in case I thought of anything else.

I got up to go and smiled at a brown-eyed girl who was walking by. She smiled back. Sometimes, when you see a beautiful girl, it breaks your heart.

~

Birmingham isn't that big and I found the hotel after asking a couple of locals for directions. Sometimes, when I most need to know, I forget if the sun rises in the East and sets in the West or vice versa. Not that I knew whether the hotel was East or West of me, but I always feel better having a sense of which way the world is spinning.

When I got to the hotel, I paced around avoiding the staff so I wouldn't have to answer any questions. Greg and Kyle finally showed up half an hour late. Greg was bleeding from the chin and they were both laughing about some show that was on TV in the 90s. I wasn't going to ask what happened, but finally gave in after it didn't seem like I'd get the story. Apparently Greg had tripped over an old lady's poodle and hit his face on an iron fence. I didn't feel bad laughing at him because he seemed to think it was funny, too.

Kyle called for his car and they accidentally brought a much nicer car than we had dropped off. I wondered who was going to tell them that it wasn't ours, but they must have known that we wouldn't be driving a car that clean and corrected their error.

We drove aimlessly through town and discussed whether we should stay in Birmingham or make our way towards Atlanta so we didn't have to drive so far the next day. Kyle was tired of driving so we decided to find a place to stay in town and leave early in the morning.

We stopped at a bar to see what would happen and four hours later we still didn't have any leads on a place to stay.

The bar was rustic and classy, but not so classy that we couldn't afford to drink. It must have been a well-kept secret because there weren't many other people inside. The bartender was wearing a cowboy hat and a bow tie. I didn't think for a minute that the locals dressed like that, but the idea was probably to cater to out-of-towners who wanted it to be true. There was one rich cowboy type playing pool with his bleach-blonde wife or mistress or whatever. I guessed he was a politician and probably had just corrupt enough character to pull it off. The type who faked a southern accent just to put people at ease when he was lying about how he supported schools and fire departments. The more he drank, the louder and angrier he got. By his sixth or seventh beer, I was positive he must have been the mayor.

"What do you think that guy does for a living?" I wanted to see if the guys were on the same page as me.

"I bet he sells used cars," Greg suggested. I hadn't thought of that, but I could picture him on a billboard with some sleazy catch-phrase. At least Greg and I agreed that he couldn't be trusted.

Kyle was a little more naive, "He looks like some kind of mega-church pastor."

On the other side of the room was the guy who country songs are written about. He looked like he had lost his wife that very day to someone more rugged and she probably took the truck when she left. I wanted to buy him a beer, but he looked like he'd had plenty. Probably couldn't even pronounce the word "beer" anymore. It was a shame the place didn't have karaoke because it was probably just what he needed.

I wondered if it's more worthwhile to surround yourself with smart people or with kind people. I know very few kind people. Maybe it depends on what you want to learn and how you want to be. I've never found much use in being smart.

When the patrons started trickling out, we wondered if "southern hospitality" was a lie. There was always the option of sleeping in the car, but we knew how that had worked out a couple nights before.

It was about 11:00 pm by the time we gave up on staying in Birmingham. The idea of driving out of town had become much more appealing so I kicked the dust off my shoes before sitting down. I was the only guy sober enough to drive and Kyle surrendered the wheel and got in the back. It was his turn to stretch out. Greg climbed in the front and it was him and I like it had been on the first days of our trip.

I took us about half way to Atlanta before I realized that Greg and Kyle were both unconscious. It was all I needed to convince me to pull over and join them. I found a truck stop and parked in a dark corner of the lot and quickly dozed off.

fifteen

I dreamed that night that my foot melted and I couldn't use it to push the brake pedal and our car was rolling backwards into traffic.

The windows were fogged over when I woke up and I couldn't remember where we were. I was alone in the car. When I got out, I found the other two in the bathroom shaving with some razors they had bought off of a trucker. It's funny how you don't notice small changes but one day you wake up and realize your beard is out of control or you have gotten fat or your kids have grown up.

"How long have you guys been up?"

"Probably an hour. We couldn't sleep through your grunting." Greg grinned smugly.

"Well, my dream wasn't as exciting as you might think. It was actually horrifying, thank you."

Kyle made some exaggerated moans to imitate my sleep noises and Greg laughed.

"Whatever," I smiled. "Will you guys get the hell out of here so I can have some privacy? I haven't pooped in days."

"You should drink more coffee." Greg had no intention of going anywhere until he had finished "man-scaping," as he called it.

Kyle finished shaving and walked outside with me to find that his car had a flat tire.

"That didn't happen while I was driving last night. I would have noticed." I was trying not to feel responsible for the setback.

"Damn...I don't have a spare."

Greg came out and asked where we were going to eat before noticing that we couldn't go anywhere. It was a relief that Kyle caught more ridicule for not carrying a spare than I got for being the last one to drive.

None of us were up for walking since we didn't know which

direction to walk or how far it was to the closest town, but someone had the brilliant idea of waiting for a car with matching wheels to show up and bumming a spare off them.

In the mean time, we laid in the grass and threw things at each other.

I discussed with my friend Aaron several years ago why it is that men use violence to build and demonstrate camaraderie and I don't think we ever came up with an answer. Well, I've heard it said that men call their friends horrible names and don't mean it while women call their friends nice names and don't mean it. I feel like I'm on the right side if that's true.

It was about two and a half hours before someone showed up with the same model of car that Kyle had and he managed to buy their spare from them for way more than it was worth. Unfortunately, he didn't have any tools either and didn't realize it until after his saviors had come and gone. Greg went and asked a trucker if we could borrow a jack and a lug wrench and we were back on road in half an hour.

Though on our first day with Kyle it had looked like we'd get to North Carolina in three days easily, I was starting to doubt we'd make the coast by that night. We resolved not to stop for beers or girls and to speed through the day and into the night if we had to. Greg and I weren't really in a hurry because there was nothing for us in North Carolina that we didn't already have except maybe the ocean. I guess we were attracted to the idea of not having to sleep another night in the car.

The miles flew by at first with only one short stop for food and gas. It was raining again, but we were glad to be screaming across Georgia at 85 miles per hour. Atlanta put us even further behind whatever schedule we were on because it really was true "what they say about Atlanta traffic."

We took I-20 out of the city and got hung up again by the State Patrol just short of the South Carolina border. I was actually surprised our luck had lasted as long as it did with Kyle pushing his car as fast as it could go since Denver. I didn't really care what happened as long as we weren't stranded and Kyle was happy to get off with only a $170 ticket that his parents would end up paying anyway. The cop started to hassle Greg, too, for the pipe that was sticking out of his front pocket, but some dispatcher on the other side of the state said something into his ear and he hurried off to save the day.

The exchange didn't slow Kyle down at all and we hit the

pavement in South Carolina at close to 90. Greg was wondering out loud how hard it would be to convince a prospective employer that one had a degree in...whatever, and whether the hiring manager would look into such claims or just take your word for it. I think the conversation actually started out with what we'd do when everything settled down and we were forced to look for jobs again. It seems like even to this day in the age of computers and simple research, I still hear stories about doctors losing their licenses because their paperwork turned out to be homemade. Someday I'll probably see Greg on TV successfully impersonating an astrophysicist. The story would be on the odds of our planet colliding with an asteroid that would wipe out humanity and Greg would be polled as an expert in the field. Knowing him, he'd throw self-preservation to the wind and have a fun time telling the reporter that we will surely collide with that very asteroid in a matter of hours and to rush home and kiss her husband and kids goodbye.

Kyle suggested that Greg just go to school and earn a degree in lieu of putting the time and effort and risk into pulling off such a heist. I was on Greg's side just for the sake of tricking the house and getting away with it. It worked for that guy who they made that movie about. Although you never get away with it permanently. Even Robin Hood died poor and alone after his beloved was killed for getting wrapped up in his lifestyle. On a long enough time line, it always catches up. But, by then you're on to the next scam. The more I thought about it, the more I knew that Greg wasn't a con and couldn't keep up the act for long enough. At least he could get a good start which is more than I could do. None of us guys in the car had the personality or the character to lie for a living, but it was entertaining to consider the possibilities for a moment. I wondered just for a second why we look up to guys who get rich by deceit, but the idea seemed like too heavy of a subject to give much thought to at the time, so I left it alone and stayed with the discussion.

The conversation got heated when Kyle asked whether we thought it was hypocritical to make money investing in a company that manufactures military arms if you think war is wrong. No one was bothered by the question, but starting a discussion of that nature is bound to bring out everyone's politics. The issue was essentially whether it's unethical to profit from something you disagree with and on the surface we all agreed that it is. The problem is that everything you buy and every place you shop says something about what you believe or will allow and so many people patronize businesses that they wouldn't support outright. For example, if you believe that eating meat is a moral issue, as many vegetarians do, are you bound by your beliefs not to shop at grocery stores that sell meat because you'd be helping to perpetuate the problem? I've heard of people boycotting national restaurant chains because they disagree with one of the CEO's beliefs. Isn't that the same thing. On the other hand, if none of us "supported" anyone who didn't subscribe to the same morals as us, would anything ever get done? It wouldn't, and maybe that's a case for not letting your beliefs dictate where you'll spend your money or how you'll make your money. Of course, there must be some middle ground, but I'm one who likes to have clearly drawn lines. A friend of mine once considered working for a company where customers can rent-to-own furniture and electronics. He didn't follow through because he believed the concept was manipulative and made poor people poorer. I wonder if every job has some element like that. A guy could pass on every job opportunity because the company is in the business to make money which, by definition, takes money away from the customer.

It had been dark for hours when we crossed into North Carolina. Kyle's parents lived on the coast in Wilmington so we still had about 80 miles to go. We stopped one last time for gas to be sure we'd make it. Greg went in like he always did and I pumped the gas while Kyle stayed in the car and laid his head back.

Greg came running out and pointed something at me and suddenly my face was wet. I was too surprised to do anything at first, but when it happened again, I ducked behind the gas pump to get away.

"What the hell are you doing?" I tried to yell at him without showing him my face again.

"I bought a water gun, Man!"

"Dude! It's the middle of Winter!" I wished I'd stayed in the car with Kyle. I think Greg's level of insanity was directly proportional to our distance from Oregon. On a scale of dull to crazy, everyone thinks they're normal and that everyone else is too far one way or the other.

I'm not so much of a bummer that I can't enjoy a good water fight (even in February) so when I got between Greg and the food mart, I ran in and bought my weapon.

Kyle just shook his head (probably jealous that he wasn't having as much fun as us) while Greg and I chased each other around until a group of Red Hat Ladies got caught in the crossfire. I didn't know sweet old women could cuss.

It was the most exercise I'd gotten since I quit my job and it felt good to run around a bit.

"You put up a hell of a fight," Greg laughed.

"You taught me everything I know about acting crazy in public," I poked back with a smile.

Back on the road, Kyle was nice enough to turn on the heat. I told him more than asking that I was going to borrow some clothes when we got to his parents house. I probably would have anyway since mine were sitting on a bench in Wyoming, but having wet clothes was a better reason to need new ones than just not owning any.

We rolled into Wilmington after midnight. It looked like a town I'd been to before, but I was sure I hadn't. Kyle pointed out where he'd gone to school and where he had his first job as we drove through town towards his parents house. It was well after midnight and they hadn't waited up. I wondered if they even knew he was coming. Greg and I slept on Kyle's bedroom floor rather than be the strangers on the couch when his mom came out in the morning. I secretly hoped his parents would be gone to work or wherever before I was up so I'd have a chance to take a shower before meeting them.

sixteen

I woke up on the floor next to Greg after another strange dream. Kyle was already out of the room and I could hear talking downstairs. I tried to clean myself up in the bathroom without helping myself to their things too much. I didn't want to look like a complete hobo and scare Mom and Dad.

My fears weren't realized when I went downstairs because Kyle was talking to another kid his age. His parents had left for work hours ago and wouldn't be home until after dark. It was about 10:00 although I thought it was much later by how dismal it looked outside.

Kyle's friend David had come over to catch up. I realized I'd never asked Kyle how long he'd been away from home, but it was over a month and I expected we'd be meeting a lot of his long lost friends wanting to reunite. He was speaking fast again now that he had someone new to talk to. I didn't recognize some of the stories he told and wondered how many were made up. The ones that I was a part of were fairly accurate, probably because he thought I'd expose him if he made up details that I knew were false.

David pulled some eggs out of the fridge and started cooking breakfast while Kyle sat on a stool and told of beautiful girls in Alabama and State Troopers in Georgia. I wondered if David was related or just comfortable enough to help himself to the food.

I wondered if a chicken omelet would be non-kosher for the same reason that a cheeseburger isn't kosher.

Greg came down in just a towel as David's breakfast was ready and I was pleased to find that he'd cooked enough for all of us.

"Oh, good, you figured out how to use the shower," Kyle didn't seem a bit annoyed that Greg would make himself at home.

"Most people don't realize that you have to pull up on that one thing while pushing down on the other."

We ate eggs and bacon while Kyle finished catching up with David. I once dated a girl who hated bacon for its taste and for its tendency to make everything in the building smell. Needless to say, we didn't date for long.

After breakfast David had to leave and Greg and I squeezed into some of Kyle's clothes. Fortunately, tight pants were in style at the time. We both used Kyle's phone to call home and Greg learned that his truck had sold. His parents would send the check through the mail so we'd have to stay in Wilmington for a couple of days to wait for it. There would be enough to throw a few hundred at a cheap car and buy some thrift store clothes. Meanwhile we would stay with Kyle if his parents didn't object.

My parents were glad to hear from me and I talked to them both for a while. Dad had been working too much as usual. They thought it was so nice that I'd found a friend to stay with in "North Dakota" (I didn't correct them). Mark Twain said that "God created war so Americans would learn geography," but it didn't help us learn about our homeland. Really, the average American probably couldn't even tell you which countries we were at war with, let alone point to them on a map. That's probably why we're so afraid of the world - because we don't know which countries we're fighting with and it's safer to suspect all of them than trust the wrong ones. I've found through most of my travels that no one has a problem with American tourists. It's our government they don't like. In fact, most places prefer to deal with American tourists because our wealth and our inability to say no are a lethal combination. I once worked with a Peruvian who thought it was bizarre that Americans think they have to be friends with everyone they meet. He didn't hide his dislike for some of our other coworkers and everyone was very uncomfortable about it. But he made a good point. Americans will be nice to someone they don't like rather than risk the awkward situation of having to admit that there's a problem. It's fantasy. I wonder where we learned that it's unacceptable to dislike people. No wonder it's becoming illegal to offend certain groups.

Kyle took us to the beach that afternoon and we watched toddlers dip their feet in the cold ocean and then cry because they got wet. Kids are completely illogical.

Greg had never seen the Atlantic and I'd only seen it

through the window of a plane. It looked a lot like the Pacific. It was still raining and the birds were trying to push against the wind. I wondered where they had to get. I wondered if they knew they were birds.

I was tired of getting wet and convinced the guys to pop into a coffee shop near the beach. I didn't want coffee, but it looked warm inside. It's been suggested that the cafe culture stemmed not out of a want for coffee, but rather want for a warm place to sit and discuss ideas. I didn't care whether the ideas flowed that afternoon. I was more interested in drying off and having a muffin.

Greg and Kyle were discussing whether the federal government could benefit from the legalization and taxation of certain drugs. I didn't have a strong opinion on the subject, but I wondered how it would affect my life if the people around me were under the influence more often than they already were. The Irish guy running the cafe sat down and shared his opinion which lined up well with Greg's. It must have been an Irish thing. Their point of view was that it's quite arbitrary which drugs are outlawed and which ones are sold everywhere and to people of any age. Kids can buy coffee and spray paint, but adults can't buy marijuana. I'm still not convinced one way or another even as I'm writing this and the prohibition of marijuana has ended in some states. Alcohol was once just as criminal and just as fiercely fought over. I wonder if folks will someday be able to get medical cards allowing the use of hallucinogenic mushrooms. Of course, it will always be profitable for doctors with questionable ethics to write a prescription to a patient who wants to use a drug recreationally but needs a legal avenue. I've been told the slippery slope argument is a logical fallacy, but I think it's valuable for predicting the future, if not for declaring a thing to be good or bad - right or wrong. Some religions require the use of certain illicit drugs and, in the past, others have required things as unthinkable as murder or the use of prostitutes.

Maybe drugs should be used to treat character flaws - marijuana for those who are too motivated, caffeine for those who aren't. A friend and I used to toy around with the idea of making everything legal and allowing natural consequences to play the role of law enforcement. Of course, it would never work because people don't care about how their decisions affect others.

Greg and Kyle and I never came to any conclusion because that's not what discussions of this nature are about. Really, it's useless for everyone to agree on the specifics because there would be nothing to talk about.

I paid for a cup of tea because I thought I could enjoy it with less effort and less doctoring than if I'd bought a coffee.

When the rain let up, we walked back to the car and Kyle drove us to his house.

His parents were both home from work and they welcomed us. Kyle looked like his mom. His ability to talk for hours obviously came from his dad and his mom graciously stood by while the two talk back and forth with increasing intensity.

Sleeping that night was more comfortable as Greg and I both had a couch and clean clothes to sleep in. I was less tired after getting a good night's sleep the night before. My mind wandered across the country and I thought of the details of our trip. It had been less than two weeks, but the amount of content made it feel like double. I wondered where we'd go from here because any movement back towards the Pacific would be backtracking. There was a lot of East coast to see. I realized that our adventure really had nothing to do with location as everything that happened could have happened anywhere. Maybe next time we'll just drive in circles around Oregon and look for trouble. But then, something about being in a new place makes the events louder. Getting lost in Jerusalem feels a lot different than getting lost ten miles from your house. Maybe just because it's easier to get help when you're close to home.

I forgot what I was thinking about and tried to backtrack.

I remembered that on our way back to Kyle's house that day Greg and I talked about getting jobs for a week in Wilmington. I wondered what a guy could do for a week in North Carolina to make some money. Maybe we would start a traveling business and stay on the road forever. I thought about a book I'd read in high school where the narrator traveled from town to town and was able to get a new job almost daily. Managers these days want to hire someone who will pass a background check and promise to come back the next day.

As I drifted off, my entrepreneurial ideas became more bizarre. The last business I remember deciding to start that night involved selling survival hammocks door-to-door that would double as rope for rappelling down a cliff or out of a window in an emergency.

seventeen

The next day was relaxing. We spent most of the day at Kyle's home and started to regain a sense of normalcy. Two more of his friends came and visited on their lunch breaks and we passed the time watching a show I'd never seen where two brothers turned nice cars into disappointing cars that no one would be proud to drive.

It was the first day of our trip that we didn't spend any money. I wondered if it had worked out for Kyle to bum some cash off his parents. He didn't seem in any hurry to get back to Colorado so maybe he hadn't asked them yet.

Greg used the computer to look for used cars that were in good enough shape to get us out of town, but poor enough that the owner couldn't ask too much. I thought about what people did in the 30s when there weren't any 25 year old cars to buy for their teenagers. The concept was ridiculous on several levels.

As romantic as the idea was, we couldn't afford any of the hippy vans that were for sale locally but there were a few Hondas that looked like they still had a hundred miles or so left in them. Greg emailed a couple guys before Kyle remembered that his stoned friend Peter was selling an early Mazda with no stereo for a few hundred dollars.

I think I should describe here a car shopping pet peeve I've had as long as I've been a driver. When putting a "for sale" sign in a car and parking it on the side of a busy thoroughfare, most sellers leave out the bit of information most important to the sale. In my opinion, the largest number visible should not be the seller's phone number, but the price of the vehicle. I am much more likely to stop and look for a phone number if I like the price than I am to stop and look for a price because I like the phone number.

We met Peter at his shack and politely listened to the sales pitch. There were more things wrong with the car than I can remember. He obviously felt bad for asking anything at all for the car but he needed to pay rent and buy a new cell phone, not necessarily in that order. Greg was better at haggling than I, but you feel bad trying to talk a friend of a friend down, so, after test driving it, we agreed to pay the $400 when Greg's check came.

~

The rest of the weekend was spent in much the same fashion. We never felt like Kyle's parents were getting tired of having us around, or maybe they were just good actors. If they were anything like my parents, they liked their house being the place where everyone hung out because they knew we were staying out of trouble.

We took a day trip to Raleigh on Sunday and Kyle paid for everything. He knew the city well enough to keep us from getting lost and to show us the best places to waste money and time.

When the rain let up, we walked through the streets. The sidewalks were uneven and my pants got wet from stepping in puddles.

Here, Kyle had the advantage of being comfortable and in a familiar place, and being the tour guide gave him ample opportunity to do his favorite thing: talk. He told us about a cousin of his who lived in Raleigh for just long enough to get banned from every bar in town. Apparently the guy was smart enough to make friends, but not smart enough to know who was worth befriending. Of course, it was never his fault. Just the victim of being on the wrong side when a fight started or when someone left without paying their tab.

On our way back out of town, we got caught up in some traffic when a motorcyclist ran his bike into a UPS truck. The wreck wasn't blocking the road, but everyone had to slow down and see if they could spot any blood or guts. The biker was still laying on the ground when we passed. I figured he was probably drunk like everyone else on the road. The UPS driver seemed more concerned about his delivery schedule than the damage.

~

The check came on Monday and we went straight to the bank then to a local second-hand store for pants and long shirts. Greg spent $10 on a trendy stocking cap, but it was his money. We met with Peter that afternoon and handed most of the rest of the money over. I didn't think the car would even make it out of his driveway. Who knows if he ever paid the rent. The place couldn't have been rented by a legitimate company the way it was falling apart. I think even North Carolina has building codes.

We had a car again and were free to move as far as it would take us, but after being spoiled all weekend, we were reluctant to forfeit Kyle's hospitality. We stayed another two nights under the guise of "planning our next move."

When Kyle's dad started asking where we were going next, we thought it was time to take the hint. At about the same time, Kyle began talking about what was waiting for him back in Denver. Nothing, I assumed, but he probably thought he had to get back to that hostel and post another rideshare ad.

We left that afternoon, Tuesday, and drove North up the coast. Kyle was the first friend we'd met on the road who I actually was going to miss. I would, however, appreciate the more peaceful ride and the increased ease of sleeping with only two guys in the car.

Greg and I talked about being carnies as we drove through the rain. It didn't occur to us that the carnival probably didn't operate in the middle of Winter. Although, now that I think about it, those guys have to feed their drug habit somehow, so maybe they do run year-round.

We made it as far as Norfolk, Virginia that night and decided to sleep in the car. The rain came in through the doors and windows and seemingly even from underneath us. We'd had enough foresight to pick up a couple cheap blankets in Wilmington when we were buying clothes a couple days before. Kyle had sent us off with some beers that we drank before falling asleep. We talked about what people in New York did for fun - probably danced at night clubs and went to art exhibits. The same kinds of things people in Portland did, but the New Yorkers probably had nicer clothes and drank more expensive wine.

I wondered if anyone had ever researched which populations within the U.S. were more likely to travel outside of their home state. There are some places where you can see everything right at home that you would see if you traveled thousands of miles across the country. Then I thought maybe those were exactly the types of people who travel more. Maybe seeing how many ways the world can be without going far encourages people to go further. Likewise, if traveling 100 miles in any direction from your house yields no new possibilities, you're probably less likely to bother going any further. I wondered if people who grew up in, say, Greenland before the age of photos and airplanes just assumed that the whole world was covered in snow.

We slept easily that night in a parking lot on the coast. In the morning, some kind of ranger or security guard told us that we couldn't camp there and moved us down the road. He didn't realize he was several hours late and we'd already "camped."

eighteen

The next morning found us pushing further North after our armed wake up call. I suggested that we visit Andrew if we ever made it through Ohio and we planned to swing that way if Greg could find the paper where he'd scrawled Andrew's information. It rained on and off and we ran into traffic in every town of more than a few thousand. Everyone's packed together more tightly on the East coast, so even drivers with short commutes plug up the overworked highways.

We didn't realize we were going to Washington DC until it was too late. The city was more majestic than I'd expected and the traffic more horrendous. It took us most of an hour to get into town by surface streets. I'd never been there and wanted to get a better look than the freeway would have offered, so Greg humored me and took the scenic route. I predicted that there were more people visiting from out of town than actually lived locally.

Most of the time, I'm not an outwardly patriotic person because I'm too distracted by other things to realize how fortunate I am, but I was proud to know that my country had a beautiful capitol. Many countries have ugly capitols destroyed by war and never rebuilt, but we've generally made sure to keep our wars out of the home court - at least since the war of 1812. Maybe that's why we're so prosperous - we never have to start from scratch like Germany did and like the entire Middle East does every few years.

We found a place to park on Pennsylvania Ave. so we could go for a walk and ended up taking a picture for an old couple in front of the Big Man's house. I was amused at the thought of people taking pictures of themselves and their families in front of my home in Dallas.

I bought my sister a souvenir trinket that I knew she wouldn't like and worked on my story about what happened to the CD collection she'd made me before we left.

"They were confiscated by the police and we were lucky not to get jail time for carrying pirated merchandise," I'd tell her. It's frowned on these days to bootleg intellectual property because the movie and record companies want trillions of dollars in profit instead of just billions. That was probably the story I'd go with. Or we'd donated them to a 12 year old in Tennessee who thought that country music was the only kind. She might be more proud of that.

The novelty of DC only entertained us for so long. I've never been a very good tourist. Soon, we were fighting worse traffic to get out than we'd encountered coming in. The secret must have been out that the capitol is a sand trap of high school field trippers and Asian tourists. I have nothing against Asians, but it's suspicious that they're more interested in American history than Americans are.

We took the 270 Northwest out of DC in order to avoid Baltimore and cut north on 81 into Pennsylvania.

Just west of Harrisburg, as it was getting dark, Greg and I had another run in with the police. To save money, we hadn't bothered to register the car back in North Carolina and were pulled over for having expired plates along with with speeding and having a tail light out. I was driving and couldn't produce a registration or proof of insurance, but maybe it was a normal occurrence in Pennsylvania because the officer let us go after we promised to get our paperwork sorted out, slow down, and fix the light. The whole event made my thumbs itch and I wondered if it's better to have multiple violations so that the cop will prefer to let you go rather than do a stack of paperwork. Maybe we just had innocent faces. Or maybe he knew that anyone with as dilapidated of a car as us couldn't afford the fine. I've heard it said that drivers from out of state are given more leniency because they'd be harder to track down if they didn't show up or pay up. Then again, I've heard that cops aren't as nice to non-locals and will throw the book at you. We probably just got lucky and the policeman was trying to get home to his wife.

We stopped in Harrisburg for the night with no intention of legalizing our ownership of the Mazda. It was colder and raining harder than it had for our entire trip so far, but we got out of the car for long enough to run into a busy-looking pub on the edge of town. Soon we discovered why it was so busy. Thursday was three dollar pizza night and we patiently waited over an hour for our dinner. When a whole pizza is three bucks, you wait for as long as it takes. I think they used Campbell's tomato soup for the pizza sauce, but, as has been said a thousand times before, even when pizza's not very good...it's still pretty good.

One guy two tables over was getting increasingly agitated as he got hungrier and was swearing at the waitress after 45 minutes. I've always found it to be awkward when someone gets angry in public at something unimportant. I used to play pool with a friend who would throw his stick on the floor of the bar when he missed a shot. Mostly, I was embarrassed for the guy for not being able to control himself. There are a lot of things in this world that we can't control, but we should at least have self-control. Some people can't even do that.

Eventually the drunk guy's pizza came and he stormed out because it didn't have pineapple on it. I wondered how he survived into his forties with such a short temper and a distorted view of reality.

Greg and I were happy to drink beers and stay warm while we waited. There was some big game on TV and everyone in the bar felt somehow involved because one of the teams was from their state. I've never understood how being from the same place as some celebrities who play a game for a living makes you and them a unit. I guarantee no one on that TV would have recognized anyone in that bar if they'd passed on the street. Still, it was good to be part of a room full of people who could agree on the importance of something. And maybe it was important. No one will remember that game in 50 years, but no one will remember much about our pop culture or politics either, so who's to say what really matters.

I talked to a lady the other day who had been married for 70 years and she didn't say anything about what they ate for dinner or what car they drove or who they voted for. The thing she thought most important to tell me was that "it's never worth it to argue." I disagreed in my head at the time, but she was probably right.

Before going back to the car, we stood outside under the awning and smoked our pipes with a guy who had flown helicopters in Vietnam before coming back home and working in a hospital. He said that after seeing so much violence, the only thing he could do to keep from killing himself was to find a job helping people who were sick or hurt. I believed all of his stories because he was drunk and had no reason to lie. I thought maybe he had found the secret to leading a fulfilling life - to help other people.

Later, Greg and I would talk about the importance of spending time with older men and gleaning wisdom rather than making the same mistakes that have already been made. We agreed that, really, the only two ways to learn a lesson are by screwing up and recovering or by taking the advice of someone who's been there. I wondered what the world would look like if each and every person didn't have to make the same mistake that everyone else has made. It made me think of friends and family members who had trusted their loved ones for years, but would ignore any advice regarding the most important decision of their life. Love is a funny thing, I guess, and I've stopped bothering to tell someone I care about when I think that they're marrying the wrong person. Universally and without fail it's the one time that they won't listen. Fortunately or unfortunately, divorce is so prolific today that it's easy to get out when they realize that everyone was right. When I have a daughter, I hope she ignores my advice about which car to buy, or which classes to take, or what color to paint her bedroom, but not about who she'll vow to spend the rest of her life with.

We slept in the car again and, even though it was smaller than Dave, it was more suited for sleeping. Both front seats leaned back almost completely horizontal and we didn't have anything in the back seats that got in the way. Even the steering wheel adjusted up away from the knees of the driver when it was time to get comfortable.

Apparently, someone thought we were dead because a few hours into sleeping, some firefighters knocked on our door and said that they'd been called out to check on a couple people slumped over in a car. It boggled my mind that someone driving by thought we would lean our seats back and wrap up with blankets before dying. I was glad the police hadn't come out because they probably would have made a thing of our lack of registration and insurance again. Greg drove us a couple blocks south to a less trafficked area and no one bothered us for the rest of the night.

We woke up less than rested and cold. I offered to drive and took us North to I-80 and West again towards Ohio, but not before stopping so Greg could get a coffee. I got one, too, just to have something hot to drink and we talked about the state of public education. Greg thought that people aren't really equal and that, under the current system, everyone is held down to the level of the dumbest kid. I thought the idea was interesting, so I kept him talking as we drove through the rain and across Pennsylvania.

"I'm not saying that people don't have equal rights," he clarified, "we just really aren't equal. It's almost communistic to say that everyone has the same potential and can be whatever they want to be and I think it's a disservice to children to let them believe that they can have a job that their personality and IQ would never fit." He talked about how in countries like Sweden, kids pick a career in high school and start their training before graduation.

"So you don't think I'll be an astronaut?" I joked because I didn't know what to say.

He went on to describe how the curriculum and the required level of competency have fallen so sharply that all one has to do is show up to be guaranteed a passing grade. It's partly due to the ratio of students per teacher, he believed, but more than anything the problem can be traced to low expectations. If a kid doesn't want to learn or his parents don't require that he apply himself, we call it a disease and dramatically lower the minimum. If enough kids are "sick" the class slows down and the students with any level of motivation or discipline are punished by having to spend extra time on something they've already learned.

"The idea that everyone is the same has paralyzed our society. You actually benefit more these days from not trying to accomplish anything because you're guaranteed a free ride that way. Did you know that there are actually college scholarships that you can only apply for if you are overweight? Dude, some people on welfare would actually take a pay CUT if they went to work. It's rather one-sided. Try organizing a straight pride parade or a white history month. You've seen commercials on TV that use reverse sexism and no one bats an eye. It's okay to call men dumb or ugly, but you'd be run out of town if you suggested that there is anything at which men are better or more suited than women."

I wasn't feeling quite as passionate about the whole thing as he was, but he made a good point.

~

We visited Andrew that afternoon, but it wasn't as fun as when he'd been forced out of his comfort zone. His apartment was small and messy and it was obvious that he really just wanted to be playing video games.

After a couple of hours, we made an excuse to leave and got back on the road. The event made me wonder if I'd go back to working dead-end jobs and hiding from my family after getting home. I decided that letting your circumstances lead is only exciting when your circumstances are exciting. The only step Andrew took was getting on the plane for Denver. Everything from then until he flew back home was forced on him. Greg, however, was the type of guy who directed his circumstances. It's the difference between being the boss of your own life or just going where it tells you to go.

Most people don't realize it, but if you don't make a choice to do anything, you're still making a choice. If you can't decide between going to college and not going to college, not choosing is the same as choosing not to go. I've been guilty of wanting to do so many things at times that rather than committing to one and missing out on the rest, I don't pick anything and missed out on even more.

We stopped in Dayton that night and the car was making more noise than when we bought it. I wondered how much further it would get us.

I called home from a gas station and my sister picked up. I hadn't talked to her since we left. A lady who looked 60 but was probably only 40 walked up to me and asked for a cigarette while I was on the phone and I let her down. Greg was standing on the roof of our car throwing rocks at a streetlight. I expected him to break the bulb and get us in trouble, but his aim was too bad.

The homeless lady walked over to him and got what she was looking for. He gave me a look of pride that his cigarettes had come in handy. I don't think he realized or cared that she didn't give him anything in return. Maybe the experience was all he wanted to buy with his "currency."

We bought cold meals and didn't bother to heat them up. We were tired of sleeping in the car and almost tried to get a hotel until we counted how much money was left.

twenty

The next day was Friday and we decided to quit the coupe before it stranded us. The benefit of being in a college town is that most students drive a car which is on the verge of giving up. In that way, we fit right in, and we hoped to pawn ours off on some unsuspecting kid before it became worthless.

Greg drove us to the University of Dayton and we spent some hours talking to private-school types outside the campus cafeteria. Apparently the world is a very different place when Mommy and Daddy are paying for college. They were all very dull. They also had no concept of the value of money and we worked a deal with a pale kid to sell him our Mazda for $450. Presumably, his bank account was bursting with free money that would discourage him from ever having to call home and bug his busy parents.

"This car is a classic!" Greg would have done well as a salesman. "She gets 31 miles to the gallon (I was sure he made the number up) and will get up and go when you need her to (his third lie in a row)."

"Thanks, guys!"

We drove him to the bank and did the paperwork before he could change his mind. You have to be quick with these sorts of things.

After parting ways with whatever-his-name-was, we loitered around campus for a few more hours and Greg tried to convince anyone who would listen that they were being duped by the college machine and that you are not defined by how you make money. He only half believed it himself, but liked to watch teenagers squirm. They were used to being praised and stroked and flattered whenever they told a real live adult about their ambitions. We didn't pretend to care that another kid was going to school to be another lawyer. And, when sharing your goals is the go-to vehicle for impressing people, it's rattling to talk to someone who thinks your goals are dumb.

I expected to be kicked out sooner or later, but we finally left of our own accord when we got bored with the complete lack of interesting people to talk to.

We walked through town and continued our dialogue on the value or uselessness of a college education.

Greg worked his charm on a skinny redhead at a fast food joint and she gave us a big discount on some extra food that had been made "by accident." He asked her to sit with us, but the place was busy and she had already taken her break. She was probably just being nice because we were starting to look less like adventurers and more like vagabonds.

In the afternoon, we made a plan to take a Greyhound west. We found the public library and used a computer to buy tickets out of town for the next morning. We chose Portland as the general destination and resolved to get off in whatever city seemed interesting along the way. After sorting out our itinerary, we played chess with a hipster on the sidewalk outside. His name was Stephen just like every hipster in the world. Somehow Greg got him to let us sleep on the floor of his studio apartment. I was glad that Greg had a way of coming through like that when we needed a place to stay.

Stephen was in some kind of art program, but if the art on his walls was done by him, he wasn't very good. Some people think that with the advent of modern art, you can do just about anything to a canvas and call it a masterpiece, but there's still somehow a distinct line between the good and the bad. I couldn't describe the difference if I had to, but you know when you see it.

Our hip friend had some girls over that night who apparently were more impressed with his work than I was. They were drinking cheap vodka and smoking expensive cigarettes that I doubted they could really appreciate. None of them could have been older than 19.

We played a game with cards and I was reminded that outside of the art world, hipsters like the same things as everyone else. He really was a nice kid. An interesting mix of self-deprecation when things mattered and seriousness when they didn't.

One of the girls got offended when Stephen made a rude joke about women. He had apparently figured out a long time ago that girls actually like you more if you disrespect them. He was right because she spent the rest of the night obviously trying to gain his approval. That was one thing I respected Greg for - that while he was charming, it was a gentlemanly charm.

Well after midnight, the drunk girls left and Stephen drifted off while educating us on the influence of Andy Warhol on contemporary advertising. I wondered if they taught him anything worthwhile in the expensive school that he was so proud of attending.

~

We left early the next morning before Stephen was awake. Greg suggested leaving him a note, but neither of us could think of anything to say, so we didn't bother. He was probably used to bringing people home and then never seeing them again.

Stephen lived on the third floor of an old apartment building and we made it out to the street just in time to see the city bus pulling away. We had a vague idea of where the Greyhound station was so we started walking in the general direction. We passed a mother who was walking faster than her four year old kid and expecting him to keep up. It was Sunday and they looked like they were late for church.

I was hungry for real food and we stopped at a produce market to pick up some breakfast. We thought it would be cheaper to stock up on a day's worth of apples and almonds rather than buy junk food at every stop the bus driver made. The lady running the market talked us into a certain variety of mango that she said was particularly smooth. Not stringy like other types. It was fascinating to talk to someone who was so knowledgeable about and in love with the fruit business. I guess everyone has their thing. I didn't think I'd found my thing yet. Maybe I still haven't found it now as I'm writing. I was told once that I was a jack of all trades and a master of none by an old woman at a restaurant where I worked. She meant it as an insult or to motivate me to go to college and get a real job, but I took it as a compliment. It made me feel like I was adaptable and could try anything in the world. I don't see how people can pick one thing to dedicate their life to when there's so much out there. But, then, if everyone was like me, there wouldn't be experts in any field. Edison wouldn't have made the light bulb because after being an inventor for a week, he would have wanted to try something else like farming or learning the piano. Maybe when you find the thing that fulfills you, it affects you so strongly that everything else loses its appeal.

We made it to the bus station and waited for our ride. It was delayed going out because it had been delayed coming in from Columbus. I've always wondered how city buses stick so closely to a schedule when there are so many random factors that affect their punctuality. Every red light has the potential to put them several minutes behind. I guess Greyhounds have the same problem. One wreck or some construction on the highway can throw the whole system out. Greg and I didn't care about the delay, but it was interesting to note that the level of anxiety of our co-riders was in direct proportion to how well they were dressed. The business types were obviously the most distraught over being late to their destination while Greg and I and a few other apparent hobos didn't even appear to notice the delay.

When the bus finally showed up, we were last to board. We didn't realize it as we waited, but letting everyone else go first would mean that there wouldn't be two empty seats adjacent to each other and we would end up sitting several rows apart for the first leg of the trip.

I sat next to a lady who didn't speak English and was glad that I wouldn't have to maintain a pleasant conversation. For a second, I thought maybe I should learn Spanish or French and catch up with the rest of the bilingual world. It seemed like a lot of work, so instead I blamed the educational system for failing me and was content.

I guess Greg sat by a lawyer, although I don't know why a lawyer would be taking the bus. Maybe he was out of work.

I tried to sleep for the first couple hours, but I was on the outside and had nothing to lean on. We stopped after about three hours and I thought that if we stop every few hours, we'd never make it to Oregon.

It's funny how people become attached to a certain seat even when they're not assigned. I remembered being in high school and everyone would sit at the same seat every day even though there was really nothing that stated it was "their seat." Something about our natural tendency to cling to a routine. Greg didn't seem to be bound by the same nature that everyone else stuck to and sat down in the Mexican lady's seat after our first rest stop. Of course, the poor woman couldn't complain because she lacked the

English vocabulary to defend "her seat." She made her way to Greg's old spot and the lawyer looked relieved to be free from the homeless looking kid who had been grilling him about the legal strategy of defending against a DUI.

"I don't think that guy's really a lawyer," Greg pondered out loud. "Not enough of a type A personality."

We agreed that a career in law would be the easiest to fake and speculated on the percentage of practicing lawyers who were merely con artists who had accidentally taken the lie too far.

~

By the end of the day, we were rolling through Kansas. I was finally exhausted enough to sleep and didn't care whether I snored or looked like a fool with my mouth hanging open.

Greg had picked up a hunting magazine because he was baffled by the whole culture and I remember trying to fall asleep as he commented on how ridiculous it seemed to need this powerful of a gun or that expensive of a camouflaged jacket.

"I thought the point was not to be seen...not for the animal to see you and think you look remarkably like foliage."

~

At dawn we were West of Denver and I was trying to stay warm. Greg had traded me spots in the night so as not to wake me up every time he went to ask the bus driver a question.

The driver was a gray-haired woman with a fashion sense either way ahead of her time, or way behind. These things go in cycles so I can never tell if someone is too hip or not hip enough.

I don't imagine Greg could have slept at all. At least every half hour he would wonder to himself out loud about the quality lobster served in Burlington, or the population of Colorado Springs, or something equally important. Then, needing an answer, he would go pester the bus driver who would make something up. He was usually satisfied with the answer and would wake me up to tell of his new found knowledge. I learned several interesting facts that night, all of which I've forgotten.

twenty-one

We were supposed to change buses in Salt Lake City in the afternoon because ours was continuing to Sacramento then San Francisco.

At the last minute, we decided to see what would happen if we stayed on the wrong bus. These things aren't as well managed as you would think and no one noticed for several hours that we weren't supposed to be there. It was at a stop for gas in Winnemucca, Nevada that Greg was talking to the bus driver and she remembered that we had been bound for Portland.

She suffered from a range of emotions on realizing we'd taken the wrong bus, from anger at our trickery, to sorrow that we were the victims of confusion, to humor that we were off on some "unplanned" adventure.

Greg set her at ease and convinced her that it was all just a big mistake and that us two country boys didn't know how to read a bus schedule. I was almost convinced myself. The sob story worked and she promised to get us on a bus to Portland for no charge as soon as we hit Sacramento in the morning.

I slept better than night. Greg didn't have as many questions to ask the driver. He did have a conversation with the child across the aisle who couldn't have been older than nine. The kid gave Greg a run for his money on the subjects of military planes and dinosaurs. I could tell that Mom wanted her child to go to sleep, but didn't have to heart to shut down the conversation, probably more for Greg's sake than the kid's.

In Reno, I got out to pee and Greg blew a couple of dollars on a slot machine. I was only momentarily surprised to see a slot machine in a transit station. As soon as he gave up, a short old woman who looked like she smoked too much walked up to Greg's machine and won $22 in one pull. Of course, with luck like that she couldn't give up and lost the whole jackpot in another five minutes.

Greg didn't seem to mind that one more try would have made him enough money to pay for a midnight snack. He was more interested in talking to a bum with an eye-patch tattoo whose sign said, "need money for bus to Houston."

"What are you going to do when you get to Houston?"

"I don't know...probably make a new sign. This one won't be no good, Brother!" yelled the bum, louder than was necessary. I figured he was probably deaf from spending all his time in loud bus and train stations.

Greg couldn't argue with that logic and changed the subject to mermaids.

twenty-two

It was still dark when we pulled into Sacramento. Traffic was already gridlocked, but the station was far enough out of town that we avoided most of it.

Our driver delivered on her promise of free tickets and we found a corner coffee shop to stay warm in while we waited. The bus was scheduled to leave that evening.

"I wonder how long we can drag out the charity," I said, mostly to myself.

"How do you mean?"

"Well, if we missed our next bus, too, could we trade these tickets in for one departing tomorrow? Shoot, we could hang out in Sacramento for weeks!"

In the afternoon, we we migrated to a bar down the block and Greg and another patron talked about the difference between vintage and antique while he drank whiskey (Greg, that is...the other guy was drinking something fluorescent and probably toxic). I always thought the words "vintage" and "antique" were more or less interchangeable, but Greg was convinced that there were specific date ranges for each. I don't remember exactly what he thought, but it was something like '50s and before for antique and '60s and '70s for vintage. I still don't know if there's any validity to what he was saying. Of course, it must change as more things start to fall out of vintage and into antique. I have a great aunt who collects antiques - or maybe she just hasn't updated her furniture since the '50s. I thought that maybe collecting antiques has to be one of the only hobbies one can adopt accidentally. The other obvious one being auto mechanics when your car breaks down frequently and you don't have the bread to take it to a shop.

~

Within three hours of landing in Sacramento, Greg was drunk on cheap whiskey and raving about Miles Davis to anyone who would listen. We were about to get kicked out of the bar and I thought we should leave preemptively, but I was also hesitant to step outside and release the beast into the wild.

Out on the sidewalk, Greg stared too hard at a cute girl and her boyfriend noticed. He was shorter than Greg and looked like Colin Farrell so he had something to prove. Greg had a way of making boyfriends feel insecure.

"What's your problem, Man?"

"Whatever, Asshole! Keep walking!" slurred Greg. It wasn't his most clever comeback to date.

Any other time, the confrontation wouldn't have progressed past shouting. This time, the stars were aligned and Greg's inhibitions were lowered and the boyfriend's primal instincts kicked in and no one on the street (including myself) stepped in in time and Greg was too slow to get the first swing off or even to dodge the punch thrown.

I couldn't tell who was more surprised by the whole thing, but it might have been Boyfriend. He probably quickly realized (as folks often do) that his first instinct might not have been the right one. Girlfriend was less than impressed and drug him away into a stream of curses and promises and threats.

I tried not to let on that I was fascinated with seeing Greg get clocked. I wasn't glad and didn't want him to be hurt, but I watched with the same interest as anyone who sees a drunk guy go looking for trouble and find it.

The event damaged Greg's morale and I tried to be supportive even though I thought he was at fault. Everyone knows that a guy has an obligation to agree that his friend was right and the other guy was a loser or a punk. I don't know if girls operate under the same rules.

Greg's determination to get home the next day was solidified.

I, on the other hand, had begun to develop an entirely different plan. See, I was acutely aware and had been for our three weeks together that Greg was the hero of our story and I was often simply an observer along for the ride. As close as we were to Dallas, I wasn't ready to go home and the prospect of striking out on my own was becoming more appealing now that Greg was drunk AND injured AND grumpy. I knew there was still adventure to be had and wondered how I would cope without Greg's extroverted tendencies pushing us down the road.

He was mildly offended that I wouldn't be joining him on the last leg of his trip, but quickly realized that I didn't care what happened as long as it wasn't the end of the road for me.

We meandered towards the bus station while Greg nursed his swollen cheek.

He told me about guitar players he'd known who knew just enough about soloing to get themselves into trouble. "They can start a killer solo, but about halfway through, it becomes obvious that they have no idea how to finish and it either turns into a train wreck or just fades away."

It seemed ironic.

twenty-three

It was awkward to see Greg off. He graciously gave me the last of the money and I had made another couple dollars selling my bus ticket to a young couple who were heading north to watch their grandmother die of cancer.

I waved as Greg's bus pulled away which seemed unnecessary.

The wind blew through the terminal and picked up a newspaper like you see in the movies. I sat down and watched the people come and go. One old guy almost missed his bus because he put his bag down and couldn't find it. Dementia.

It had been dark and cold for an hour before Greg left. Now, two hours later, it was darker and colder and I hadn't considered where I would sleep yet. The bus station seemed cheap and I found a corner to close my eyes in. It was hard to sleep because my mind wandered.

Again, I thought about what my family would be doing. I promised myself that I would call them in the morning after I had some kind of semi-reasonable plan that they wouldn't try to talk me out of.

~

I woke up to a pair of toddlers standing a couple of feet away staring at me intently. They scattered when I smiled. I've never really figured out how to relate to kids. I think maybe you have to be their mom.

I found a pay phone and called home. No one answered, so I left a generic message. Send money.

The station was starting to bustle. Ladies in long coats dragged their bored husbands along towards family functions or wherever people go by bus.

I've never been uncomfortable with crowded places. Some people avoid them for fear of a terrorist attack or whatever. I think you're more likely to die alone. At least with people around, there's someone who can help. Although I have a friend who used to work at a restaurant and she said that one day a guy coded in the buffet line and people stepped over his lifeless body to fill their plates. That's a study in human nature, right there. Don't die when there's food, sex, or football happening. Someone dying on the floor takes a back seat to the things that are really important. I think dying and being shocked back to life could be the best thing or the worst thing. Like winning the lottery. Most people end up worse off in the end than in their former state. Too many studies have shown that folks who win large sums of money can be found impoverished again within a few months. Probably because their bad habits made them poor in the first place. Winning the lottery doesn't make you good with money just like getting married doesn't make you stop thinking other girls are pretty. Or so I've heard. Character flaws can't be cured with more of the commodity with which you've been irresponsible. When you look at it that way, it's funny to think that poor people "just need money to get out of this mess," and folks who are trying to quit smoking are "just gonna finish this pack."

I walked outside and hit a wall of cold air. The city bus was just pulling up to its stop down the block so I decided to take the opportunity to get into town. Traffic was still terrible, but I wasn't in a hurry.

An old man on the bus asked me where he could buy art supplies. He must not have been an artist for long. Or he wasn't from the area. It's never too late to start a new hobby, I guess. I think when I'm old, I'll take up clock-making.

I got out at what looked like the middle of the city - as if there could be a specific middle point in a sprawling town like Sacramento. It seemed warmer, probably because the buildings blocked the wind. They also blocked the sun and it was darker than when I'd left the station.

The homeless population was out in force and I felt like I was in the majority for the first time since leaving home. Oh, if my grandmother could see me.

I was distracted by the bigness of everything as I walked down the sidewalk and I bumped into several people. No one seemed to mind. They were just as distracted talking on cellphones and looking at their watches. One guy was actively reading the Wall Street Journal and speed-walking at the same time.

As I walked past the door of some national coffee chain, the air drew me in with smells of cinnamon and chocolate and citrus. Whatever I got didn't live up to my expectations, but it was warm inside. I wondered, again, what people do in cities. Naturally, the options are limited when you don't know anyone. Whatever. That's true anywhere, I guess.

A guy in a suit walked in and ordered a coffee like he was something important. It was some kind of magical to see how attentively he was waited on as he became more arrogant and high-maintenance. I've never understood why demanding, cocky folks are held so highly and people who are humble and kind or don't cause any problems are virtually ignored.

I used to work with a guy named Mark who was always causing problems and, therefore, was always in the bosses office. The effect was that he got to know the boss better than anyone else and they were able to connect more naturally. When he wasn't making trouble, he was always the victim of some trouble at home - some financial disaster or family emergency. Imagine my surprise when the boss was more willing to come to the aid of the guy who was irresponsible with his money and didn't know how to treat people well than to any of the employees who just did a good job and went home without making much noise.

When I was younger and first noticing this paradox, I considered making a social experiment out of it. I thought maybe I would treat people horribly for a while and see how quickly it made me rich and famous. Of course, I decided that I'd rather do the right thing than be an asshole for the sake of personal gain, but some people clearly don't have the same values. It's a shame that our culture so obviously rewards the most self-absorbed of men. Makes you wonder.

Nice guys finish last, and all that.

As I got up to leave, I promised myself that if I was ever in charge of anything important, I wouldn't reward the selfish types. It would probably put me out of business or get me sued, but, on principal, I'd rather ask someone to leave than encourage my subordinates to reward rude behavior. Ironically, I'll probably never be put in charge of anything important because for exactly this reason.

I got halfway down the block and tripped over a kid who

was unloading some audio equipment out of his van and carrying it into a bookstore. He was the type who would rather take one precarious, uncomfortable trip with everything in tow than walk back to the van once or twice to pick up another handful. I'm the same way, so I offered to help rather than watch him break all of his expensive electronics.

His name was Bobby and he was setting up for some kind of weird show with his friend Danny. They said it was a "concert," but I couldn't find any guitars or drums or much else familiar. We unloaded a keyboard and some speakers and I tried not to ask too many questions. While they were setting up, I hung out and chatted to try to get some idea of how they were going to put on a musical show without any instruments.

I was already committed to sticking around for the show when they invited me to stay. It was a good thing because there was no one else in the "audience."

Well, when they started playing, it was Danny singing and punching buttons on a laptop while Bobby played the keyboard. I still don't know what part of the music was coming from the keyboard and what was coming from the computer, but I wouldn't be surprised if it was all prerecorded and merely played back through the speakers while the two danced silently and ridiculously on the stage.

Furthermore, I couldn't classify the genre at the time. The same kind of bassy electronic music is fairly common now, but, at the time, part of me thought they were making a big, ironic joke that no one got. Not that anyone was listening. If it was a joke, I probably looked foolish clapping after each "song."

I think that's how new genres of music and art are created - by doing something extreme as a joke that then catches on with some stoned, young demographic.

~

When the boys were done goofing around on stage, I helped them load the gear back into their van and joined them for beer and burgers across the street. They told me they were from Boise and were touring the country with their act.

"Our next show is in Vegas," Bobby told me with a straight face, so I assumed he took himself somewhat seriously.

"You should come with us!" Danny suggested after enough beers to make the invitation seem rational. I laughed off the idea and asked them what they call their kind of music.

"It's original, Man. No one makes music like us." Danny was still very serious - or carrying the joke as far as he could.

"Yeah, it's revolutionary...like the Beatles," Bobby told me.

That's when I decided they were madmen and I'd ride along with them to Nevada if they would have me.

The conversation didn't stray much from their music, which I still thought was a bit...unconventional, unorganized, self-indulgent, funny, and whatever else. We ate burgers and drank beers and laughed for a couple hours and I made sure never to suggest that their music was anything less than cutting-edge. When they offered again to take me as far as Las Vegas, I agreed and thanked them.

"I'll be your biggest fan," I joked once I knew they wouldn't take my jest offensively. I used to have a friend who would call fat people fat, then say he was just joking. He didn't seem to get that it's not really a joke if the premise is true. More like satire. Maybe not even that. I don't know.

I thought they were brothers at first. They told me there had met at work and become friends before inventing their original sound. Danny, the singer, seemed to be in charge of the "band." Bobby was a year younger and might have just been along for the ride. Who knows? Not that he wasn't just as convinced as Danny - he just didn't seem to be the idea man.

~

At nine in the evening, we loaded into the van. Bobby curled up next to his keyboard in the back and let me sit up front. For the first time that evening, Danny asked me what my story was and I told him what Greg and I had been up to. Now that he felt secure in the fact that I took his art seriously, he seemed willing to let the subject rest. I got more of their story of growing up in Idaho and going to work for a retail giant to fund their expensive love for music. Danny got fired a few months ago so Bobby quit, too, and they took the opportunity to follow their dream of touring. Of course, their parents tried to be the voice of reason, but their passion couldn't be tamed. Or something like that.

The van was comfortable and the heater worked beautifully (during my great adventure that year, I came to judge vehicles by how well the heater worked).

I fell asleep mid-conversation and woke up when we stopped at a gas station so the boys could switch seats. I went in and bought something fried.

When I got back to the van, Danny told me we were past Fresno and about to make our way East once we hit Bakersfield. I wondered why their big national tour didn't include more than one show in California. I guessed it was a good thing I was at the bookstore in Sacramento or no one in California would have heard their music. Now that I was part of their posse, however, I probably didn't count.

Bobby gave me a music lesson for about the next hundred miles. He would put in a CD, play the first half of several songs, tell me about how brilliant the band was, and repeat. I hadn't heard of any of the bands and was content to be ignorant to an entire corner of the musical world. I played along well enough and he eventually let me sleep. I dreamed of an octopus that played a different instrument with each tentacle and floated above the clouds.

twenty-four

I woke up when we ran over a large rodent near the border of Nevada and Danny laughed like a villain. It was getting light. We were heading due East and, on this clear morning, the sun coming up over the mountains shone straight into my eyes if I slumped in my seat. The only way not to be blinded was to sit up straight so the visor would just guard my face.

We had been driving for over nine hours. I slept through the most recent gas stop and only realized it when I noticed that Danny was driving again. I was glad they hadn't stabbed me or rolled me for my empty wallet and left me on the side of the road.

Danny steered the van into Vegas. I expected to head towards the strip, but we stayed on the outskirts of town. Don't ask me why I thought they would be playing a legitimate venue. We had breakfast at a diner where Danny asked the manager if he would be interested in having a musical act play in the corner. I wasn't surprised when he was turned down. There wasn't really a corner to play in and, even if there was, it wasn't the type of place for the type of music. I wasn't convinced there was any place for their type of music. Maybe a garage. Or at some club in Sweden.

We finished our pancakes and eggs and got back in the van. Being turned down by the diner gave the boys a renewed drive to succeed. I'm sure they got turned down all the time. People like them love the idea of being misunderstood. It gives them an opportunity to feel disadvantaged and everyone loves an underdog.

Without an impromptu show to occupy us for the morning, we sat in a park and made faces at children. The problem with being an electronic musician is that you can't practice your instrument without a power source. Bobby reiterated several times that he wished he could rehearse for their show this afternoon, but didn't have anywhere to plug in. I kept my thoughts to myself.

I wandered off for a while while the two of them tried to write a new song. If they got arrested for looking and acting like a couple of drug freaks, I didn't want to be associated.

When I came back from my walk, Bobby was rearranging the gear in the van to make room to lay down and Danny was poking at bugs on the sidewalk.

~

The big show was scheduled for 5:00 at a coffee shop and we showed up at 4:00 to set up. I helped unload their things and found a dark corner to drink my hot chocolate.

I was confused when the show started and the two had switched positions. Danny was poking at the keyboard and Bobby was lip-syncing into the microphone and fiddling with the computer. The noise coming from the speakers was the same as it had been at the bookstore in Sacramento. If I didn't know anything else about them, I knew that they were either insane or genius. I guess in this day and age, the two are often indistinguishable. Then, maybe they always were. From Galileo to Jesus Christ to Napoleon to Picasso...there were probably as many folks who saw insanity in these men as those who saw intelligence and credibility.

Fortunately for the band - and probably by accident - the coffee shop was full of people. More amazingly, it didn't clear out when the music started. I guess people in Vegas consider anything a show and will enjoy watching as much to observe lunacy as to appreciate talent.

~

We celebrated the successful gig by going next door for whiskey after the show was over and the gear was loaded into the van.

Danny and Bobby got drunk quickly.

There was a rare, warm rain falling on the city and I didn't think we'd be going far that night. I liked the idea of spending a night in Vegas. Not to get caught up in anything that Vegas is known for, but to watch the bustle and stop in a new place for a night. Life gets confusing when you go to sleep in one spot and wake up in another for too many nights in a row.

I helped Bobby walk to the van after a few hours while Danny talked to a couple of 30-something girls. I don't think he realized that they weren't impressed, but amused.

Bobby crawled into the back of the van and fell right asleep. I sat up front in the passenger seat and let my mind wander. I thought about the time I'd spent bumming around the country. I didn't mind that I didn't own anything. It was a feeling I'd never had before.

I thought about journalists. Once in a while, you run into someone who is passionate about journalism. It never made sense to me that someone could love writing articles. Then I realized that writing isn't the substance of the job. Writing is the necessary end that requires the writer to be part of what's happening. No one loves writing an article about who won the 100-meter dash in the last Olympics, but anyone would write that article if it guaranteed free, round-trip airfare, a hotel stay, front row seats to the biggest sporting event in the world, and enough expense money to go out for steak and beer every night while you're there. You'd be mad not to. Press passes. That's what journalism is all about. I wondered if I could do it. It's somewhat appealing, the idea of traveling the world and being part of major events, only to owe somebody a 500 word article when you get home. There's probably more to it than that.

That night, I decided to go home. My adventure had spiraled beautifully. I think the longer you're on the road, the more natural madness becomes. I've never been the homesick type, but I knew at that moment that I would rather have a home than be a career wanderer. I would rather have more family and less interesting stories. And I would rather have the opportunity, at least, to stay in one place long enough to meet a girl and fall in love. I talked to a long-term vagabond once who told me that if he could do it all over again, he wouldn't.

There's something romantic about losing all sense responsibility to cooperate. I still consider it sometimes. Maybe it would be fun to go out into the world again and forget normal. To get drunk and play flute in the middle of a public park for quarters. Or, to sleep on sidewalks and eat food that someone else didn't finish. Maybe some people are better at it than others.

Shawn Mullins seems to pull it off and even make it sound ideal, but I guess that's his job. Maybe I just have different priorities.

I walked down the street knowing that Danny and Bobby would be fine without me. A bum on the sidewalk asked me for money and I gave him a dollar. I wanted to ask him if he was a bum by accident - if he'd started out on a great adventure and ran out of money, or got sick, or arrested. It was just before midnight and I stepped inside a grocery store to use the payphone. I called a cab while I watched the kid behind the counter flick a lighter.

The cab driver took me to the bus station and I slouched on a bench in the corner. I was becoming very familiar with buying Greyhound tickets and paid for my bus out of town. My ride would leave the next morning so I spent an hour talking to another traveler who had just gotten into town, then closed my eyes and slept on one more bench.

ABOUT THE AUTHOR

Tim is living the dream in the Pacific Northwest with his lovely
wife Katie. This is his first novel.